Policeman Bluejay

Policeman Bluejay

L. Frank Baum

ÆGYPAN PRESS

1907

L. Frank Baum originally published this book using the pseudonym "Laura Bancroft."

Special thanks to Michael Gray, who can be reached at the email address Lost_Gamer@comcast.net.

Policeman Bluejay
A publication of
ÆGYPAN PRESS

www.aegypan.com

To the Children

I must admit that the great success of the *Twinkle Tales* has astonished me as much as it has delighted the solemn-eyed, hard working publishers. Therefore I have been encouraged to write a new *Twinkle Book,* hoping with all my heart that my little friends will find it worthy to occupy a place beside the others on their pet bookshelves. And because the children seem to especially love the story of "Bandit Jim Crow," and bird-life is sure to appeal alike to their hearts and their imaginations, I have again written about birds.

The tale is fantastical, and intended to amuse rather than instruct; yet many of the traits of the feathered folk, herein described, are in strict accordance with natural history teachings and will serve to acquaint my readers with the habits of birds in their wildwood homes. At the same time my birds do unexpected things, because I have written a fairy tale and not a natural history.

The question is often asked me whether Twinkle and Chubbins were asleep or awake when they encountered these wonderful adventures; and it grieves me to reflect that the modern child has been deprived of fairy tales to such an extent that it does not know – as I did when a girl – that in a fairy story it does not matter whether one is awake or not. You must accept it as you would a fragrant breeze that cools your brow, a draft of sweet water, or the delicious flavor of a strawberry, and be grateful for the pleasure it brings you, without stopping to question too closely its source.

For my part I am glad if my stories serve to while away a pleasant hour before bedtime or keep one contented on a rainy day. In this way they are sure to be useful, and if a little tenderness for the helpless animals and birds is acquired with the amusement, the value of the tales will be doubled.

LAURA BANCROFT*

* L. Frank Baum wrote this book under the pseudonym "Laura Bancroft."

Chapter I

Little Ones in Trouble

"Seems to me, Chub," said Twinkle, "that we're lost."

"Seems to me, Twink," said Chubbins, "that it isn't *we* that's lost. It's the path."

"It was here a minute ago," declared Twinkle.

"But it isn't here now," replied the boy.

"That's true," said the girl.

It really *was* queer. They had followed the straight path into the great forest, and had only stopped for a moment to sit down and rest, with the basket between them and their backs to a big tree. Twinkle winked just twice, because she usually took a nap in the afternoon, and Chubbins merely closed his eyes a second to find out if he could see that long streak of sunshine through his pink eyelids. Yet during this second, which happened while Twinkle was winking, the path had run away and left them without any guide or any notion which way they ought to go.

Another strange thing was that when they jumped up to look around them the nearest trees began sliding away, in a circle, leaving the little girl and boy in a clear space. And the trees continued moving back and back, farther and farther, until all their trunks were jammed tight together, and not even a mouse could have crept between them. They made a solid ring around Twinkle and Chubbins, who stood looking at this transformation with wondering eyes.

"It's a trap," said Chubbins; "and we're in it."

"It looks that way," replied Twinkle, thoughtfully. "Isn't it lucky, Chub, we have the basket with us? If it wasn't for that, we might starve to death in our prison."

"Oh, well," replied the little fellow, "the basket won't last long. There's plenty of starve in the bottom of it, Twinkle, any way you can fix it."

"That's so; unless we can get out. Whatever do you suppose made the trees behave that way, Chubbins?

"Don't know," said the boy.

Just then a queer creature dropped from a tree into the ring and began moving slowly toward them. It was flat in shape, like a big turtle; only it hadn't a turtle's hard shell. Instead, its body was covered with sharp prickers, like rose thorns, and it had two small red eyes that looked cruel and wicked. The children could not see how many legs it had, but they must have been very short, because the creature moved so slowly over the ground.

When it had drawn near to them it said, in a pleading tone that sounded soft and rather musical:

"Little girl, pick me up in your arms, and pet me!"

Twinkle shrank back.

"My! I couldn't *think* of doing such a thing," she answered.

Then the creature said:

"Little boy, please pick me up in your arms, and pet me!"

"Go 'way!" shouted Chubbins. "I wouldn't touch you for anything."

The creature turned its red eyes first upon one and then upon the other.

"Listen, my dears," it continued; "I was once a beautiful maiden, but a cruel tuxix transformed me into this awful shape, and so must I remain until some child willingly takes me in its arms and pets me. Then, and not till then, will I be restored to my proper form."

"Don't believe it! Don't believe it!" cried a high, clear voice, and both the boy and the girl looked quickly around to see who had spoken. But no one besides themselves was in sight, and they only noticed a thick branch of one of the trees slightly swaying its leaves.

"What is a tuxix?" asked Twinkle, who was beginning to feel sorry for the poor creature.

"It is a magician, a sorcerer, a wizard, and a witch all rolled into one," was the answer; "and you can imagine what a dreadful thing that would be."

"Be careful!" cried the clear voice, again. "It is the tuxix herself who is talking to you. Don't believe a word you hear!"

At this the red eyes of the creature flashed fire with anger, and it tried to turn its clumsy body around to find the speaker. Twinkle and Chubbins looked too, but only heard a flutter and a mocking laugh coming from the trees.

"If I get my eye on that bird, it will never speak again," exclaimed the creature, in a voice of fury very different from the sweet tones it had at first used; and perhaps it was this fact that induced the children to believe the warning was from a friend, and they would do well to heed it.

"Whether you are the tuxix or not," said Twinkle, "I never will touch you. You may be sure of that."

"Nor I," declared Chubbins, stoutly, as he came closer to the girl and grasped her hand in his own.

At this the horrid thing bristled all its sharp prickers in anger, and said:

"Then, if I cannot conquer you in one way, I will in another. Go, both of you, and join the bird that warned you, and live in the air and the trees until you repent your stubbornness and promise to become my slaves. The tuxix has spoken, and her magical powers are at work. Go!"

In an instant Twinkle saw Chubbins shoot through the air and disappear among the leaves of one of the tall trees. As he went he seemed to grow very small, and to change in shape.

"Wait!" she cried. "I'm coming, too!"

She was afraid of losing Chubbins, so she flew after him, feeling rather queer herself, and a moment after was safe in the tall tree, clinging with her toes to a branch and looking in amazement at the boy who sat beside her.

Chubbins had been transformed into a pretty little bird – all, that is, except his head, which was Chubbins' own head reduced in size to fit the bird body. It still had upon it the straw hat, which had also grown small in size, and the sight that met Twinkle's eyes was so funny that she laughed merrily, and her laugh was like the sweet warbling of a skylark.

Chubbins looked at her and saw almost what she saw; for Twinkle was a bird too, except for her head, with its checked sunbonnet, which had grown small enough to fit the pretty, glossy-feathered body of a lark.

Both of them had to cling fast to the branch with their toes, for their arms and hands were now wings. The toes were long and sharp pointed, so that they could be used in the place of fingers.

"My!" exclaimed Twinkle; "you're a queer sight, Chubbins!"

"So are you," answered the boy. "That mean old thing must have 'witched us."

"Yes, we're 'chanted," said Twinkle. "And now, what are we going to do about it? We can't go home, for our folks would be scared nearly into fits. And we don't know the way home, either."

"That's so," said Chubbins, fluttering his little wings to keep from falling, for he had nearly lost his balance.

"What shall we do?" she continued.

"Why, fly around and be gay and happy," said a clear and merry voice beside them. "That's what birds are expected to do!"

Chapter II

The Forest Guardian

Twinkle and Chubbins twisted their heads around on their little feathered necks and saw perched beside them a big bird of a most beautiful blue color. At first they were a bit frightened, for the newcomer seemed of giant size beside their little lark bodies, and he was, moreover, quite fierce in appearance, having a crest of feathers that came to a point above his head, and a strong beak and sharp talons. But Twinkle looked full into the shrewd, bright eye, and found it good humored and twinkling; so she plucked up courage and asked:

"Were you speaking to us?"

"Very likely," replied the blue bird, in a cheerful tone. "There's no one else around to speak to."

"And was it you who warned us against that dreadful creature below in the forest?" she continued.

"It was."

"Then," said Twinkle, "we are very much obliged to you."

"Don't mention it," said the other. "I'm the forest policeman – Policeman Bluejay, you know – and it's my duty to look after everyone who is in trouble."

"We're in trouble, all right," said Chubbins, sorrowfully.

"Well, it might have been worse," remarked Policeman Bluejay, making a chuckling sound in his throat that Twinkle thought was meant for a laugh. "If you had ever touched the old tuxix she would have transformed you into toads or lizards. That is an old trick of hers, to get children into her power and then change them into things as loathsome as herself."

"I wouldn't have touched her, anyhow," said Twinkle.

"Nor I!" cried Chubbins, in his shrill, birdlike voice. "She wasn't nice."

"Still, it was good of you to warn us," Twinkle added, sweetly.

The Bluejay looked upon the fluttering little things with kind approval. Then he laughed outright.

"What has happened to your heads?" he asked.

"Nothing, 'cept they're smaller," replied Chubbins.

"But birds shouldn't have human heads," retorted the bluejay. "I suppose the old tuxix did that so the birds would not admit you into their society, for you are neither all bird nor all human. But never mind; I'll explain your case, and you may be sure all the birds of the forest will be kind to you."

"Must we stay like this always?" asked Twinkle, anxiously.

"I really can't say," answered the policeman. "There is said to be a way to break every enchantment, if one knows what it is. The trouble in these cases is to discover what the charm may be that will restore you to your natural shapes. But just now you must make up your minds to live in our forest for a time, and to be as happy as you can under the circumstances."

"Well, we'll try," said Chubbins, with a sigh.

"That's right," exclaimed Policeman Bluejay, nodding his crest in approval. "The first thing you must have is a house; so, if you will fly with me, I will try to find you one."

"I – I'm afraid!" said Twinkle, nervously.

"The larks," declared the bluejay, "are almost the strongest and best flyers we have. You two children have now become skylarks, and may soar so high in the air that you can scarcely see the earth below you. For that reason you need have no fear whatever. Be bold and brave, and all will be well."

He spoke in such a kindly and confident voice that both Twinkle and Chubbins gained courage; and when the policeman added: "Come on!" and flew straight as an arrow into the air above the tree-tops, the two little skylarks with their girl and boy heads followed swiftly after him, and had no trouble in going just as fast as their conductor.

It was quite a pleasant and interesting experience, to dart through the air and be in no danger of falling. When they rested on their outstretched wings they floated as lightly as bubbles, and soon a joyous thrill took possession of them and they began to understand why it is that the free, wild birds are always so happy in their native state.

The forest was everywhere under them, for it was of vast extent. Presently the bluejay swooped downward and alighted near the top of a tall maple tree that had many thick branches.

In a second Twinkle and Chubbins were beside him, their little hearts beating fast in their glossy bosoms from the excitement of their rapid flight. Just in front of them, firmly fastened to a crotch of a limb, was a neatly built nest of a grey color, lined inside with some soft substance that was as smooth as satin.

"Here," said their thoughtful friend, "is the nest that Niddie Thrush and Daisy Thrush built for themselves a year ago. They have now gone to live in a wood across the big river, so you are welcome to their old home. It is almost as good as new, and there is no rent to pay."

"It's awfully small!" said Chubbins.

"Chut-chut!" twittered Policeman Bluejay. "Remember you are not children now, but skylarks, and that this is a thrush's nest. Try it, and you are sure to find it will fit you exactly."

So Twinkle and Chubbins flew into the "house" and nestled their bodies against its soft lining and found that their friend was right. When they were cuddled together, with their slender legs tucked into the feathers of their breasts, they just filled the nest to the brim, and no more room was necessary.

"Now, I'll mark the nest for you, so that everyone will know you claim it," said the policeman; and with his bill he pecked a row of small dots in the bark of the limb, just beside the nest. "I hope you will be very happy here, and this afternoon I will bring some friends to meet you. So now good-bye until I see you again."

"Wait!" cried Chubbins. "What are we going to eat?"

"Eat!" answered the bluejay, as if surprised. "Why, you may feast upon all the good things the forest offers – grubs, beetles, worms, and butterfly-eggs."

"Ugh!" gasped Chubbins. "It makes me sick to just think of it."

"What!"

"You see," said Twinkle, "we are not *all* birds, Mr. Bluejay, as you are; and that makes a big difference. We have no bills to pick up the things that birds like to eat, and we do not care for the same sort of food, either."

"What *do* you care for?" asked the policeman, in a puzzled voice.

"Why, cake and sandwiches, and pickles, and cheese, such as we had in our basket. We couldn't *eat* any live things, you see, because we are not used to it."

The bluejay became thoughtful.

"I understand your objection," he said, "and perhaps you are right, not having good bird sense because the brains in your heads are still human brains. Let me see: what can I do to help you?"

The children did not speak, but watched him anxiously.

"Where did you leave your basket?" he finally asked.

"In the place where the old witch 'chanted us."

"Then," said the officer of the forest, "I must try to get it for you."

"It is too big and heavy for a bird to carry," suggested Twinkle.

"Sure enough. Of course. That's a fact." He turned his crested head upward, trying to think of a way, and saw a black speck moving across the sky.

"Wait a minute! I'll be back," he called, and darted upward like a flash.

The children watched him mount into the sky toward the black speck, and heard his voice crying out in sharp, quick notes. And before long Policeman Bluejay attracted the other bird's attention, causing it to pause in its flight and sink slowly downward until the two drew close together.

Then it was seen that the other bird was a great eagle, strong and sharp-eyed, and with broad wings that spread at least six feet from tip to tip.

"Good day, friend eagle," said the bluejay; "I hope you are in no hurry, for I want to ask you to do me a great favor."

"What is it?" asked the eagle, in a big, deep voice.

"Please go to a part of the forest with me and carry a basket to some friends of mine. I'll show you the way. It is too heavy for me to lift, but with your great strength you can do it easily."

"It will give me pleasure to so favor you," replied the eagle, politely; so Policeman Bluejay led the way and the eagle followed with such mighty strokes of its wings that the air was sent whirling in little eddies behind him, as the water is churned by a steamer's paddles.

It was not very long before they reached the clearing in the forest. The horrid tuxix had wriggled her evil body away, to soothe her disappointment by some other wicked act; but the basket stood as the children had left it.

The eagle seized the handle in his stout beak and found it was no trouble at all for him to fly into the air and carry the basket with him.

"This way, please – this way!" chirped the bluejay; and the eagle bore the precious burden safely to the maple tree, and hung it upon a limb just above the nest.

As he approached he made such a fierce fluttering that Twinkle and Chubbins were dreadfully scared and flew out of their nest, hopping from limb to limb until they were well out of the monstrous bird's way. But when they saw the basket, and realized the eagle's kindly act, they flew toward him and thanked him very earnestly for his assistance.

"Goodness me!" exclaimed the eagle, turning his head first on one side and then on the other, that both his bright eyes might observe the child-larks; "what curious creatures have you here, my good policeman?"

"Why, it is another trick of old Hautau, the tuxix. She found two children in the forest and enchanted them. She wanted to make them toads, but they wouldn't touch her, so she couldn't. Then she got herself into a fine rage and made the little dears half birds and half children, as you see them. I was in a tree near by, and saw the whole thing. Because I was sorry for the innocent victims I befriended them, and as this basket belongs to them I have asked you to fetch it to their nest."

"I am glad to be of service," replied the eagle. "If ever you need me, and I am anywhere around," he continued, addressing the larks, "just call me, and I will come at once."

"Thank you," said Twinkle, gratefully.

"We're much obliged," added Chubbins.

Then the eagle flew away, and when he was gone Policeman Bluejay also bade them good-bye.

"I'll be back this afternoon, without fail," he said. "Just now I must go and look over the forest, and make sure none of the birds have been in mischief during my absence. Do not go very far from your nest, for a time, or you may get lost. The forest is a big place; but when you are more used to it and to your new condition you can be more bold in venturing abroad."

"We won't leave this tree," promised Twinkle, in an earnest voice.

And Chubbins chimed in with, "That's right; we won't leave this tree until you come back."

"Good-bye," said the policeman.

"Good-bye," responded Twinkle and Chubbins.

So the bluejay darted away and was soon lost to sight, and Twinkle and Chubbins were left alone to seriously consider the great misfortune that had overtaken them.

Chapter III

The Child-Larks

"Folks will be worried about us, Twink," said Chubbins.

"'Course they will," Twinkle replied. "They'll wonder what has become of us, and try to find us."

"But they won't look in the tree-tops."

"No."

"Nor think to ask the birds where we are."

"Why should they?" enquired Twinkle. "They can't talk to the birds, Chub."

"Why not? We talk to them, don't we? And they talk to us. At least, the p'liceman and the eagle did."

"That's true," answered Twinkle, "and I don't understand it a bit. I must ask Mr. Bluejay to 'splain it to us."

"What's the use of a p'liceman in the forest?" asked Chubbins, after a moment's thought.

"I suppose," she replied, "that he has to keep the birds from being naughty. Some birds are just awful mischiefs, Chub. There's the magpies, you know, that steal; and the crows that fight; and the jackdaws that are saucy, and lots of others that get into trouble. Seems to me P'liceman Bluejay's a pretty busy bird, if he looks after things as he ought."

"Prob'ly he's got his hands full," said Chubbins.

"Not that; for he hasn't any hands, anymore than we have. Perhaps you ought to say he's got his wings full," suggested Twinkle.

"That reminds me I'm hungry," chirped the boy-lark.

"Well, we've got the basket," she replied.

"But how can we eat cake and things, witched up as we are?"

"Haven't we mouths and teeth, just the same as ever?"

"Yes, but we haven't any hands, and there's a cloth tied over the top of the basket."

"Dear me!" exclaimed Twinkle; "I hadn't thought of that."

They flew together to the basket and perched upon the edge of it. It seemed astonishingly big to them, now that they were so small; but Chubbins remarked that this fact was a pleasant one, for instead of eating all the good things the basket contained at one meal, as they had at first intended, it would furnish them with food for many days to come.

But how to get into the basket was the thing to be considered just now. They fluttered around on every side of it, and finally found a small place where the cloth was loose. In a minute Chubbins began clawing at it with his little feet, and Twinkle helped him; so that gradually they managed to pull the cloth away far enough for one of them to crawl through the opening. Then the other followed, and because the big basket was not quite full there was exactly room for them to stand underneath the cloth and walk around on top of a row of cookies that lay next to a row of sandwiches.

The cookies seemed enormous. One was lying flat, and Chubbins declared it seemed as big around as the dining-table at home.

"All the better for us," said Twinkle, bending her head down to nibble at the edge of the cookie.

"If we're going to be birds," said Chubbins, who was also busily eating as best he could, "we ought to be reg'lar birds, and have bills to peck with. This being half one thing and half another doesn't suit me at all."

"The witch wasn't trying to suit us," replied Twinkle; "she was trying to get us into trouble."

"Well, she did it, all right," he said.

It was not so hard to eat as they had feared, for their slender necks enabled them to bend their heads low. Chubbins' hat fell off, a minute later, and he wondered how he was going to get it on his head again.

"Can't you stand on one foot, and use the other foot like a hand?" asked Twinkle.

"I don't know," said he.

"The storks stand on one leg," continued the girl. "I've seen 'em in pictures."

So Chubbins tried it, and found he could balance his little body on one leg very nicely. For if he toppled either way he had but to spread his wings and tail feathers and so keep himself from falling. He picked up his hat with the claws of his other foot and managed to put it on by ducking his head.

This gave the boy-lark a new idea. He broke off a piece of the cookie and held it in his claw while he ate it; and seeing his success Twinkle followed his example, and after a few attempts found she could eat very comfortably in that way.

Having had their luncheon – and it amazed Chubbins to see how very little was required to satisfy their hunger – the bird-children crept out of the basket and flew down to the twig beside their nest.

"Hello!" cried a strange voice. "Newcomers, eh?"

They were so startled that they fluttered a moment to keep from tumbling off the limb. Then Twinkle saw a furry red head sticking out of a small hollow in the trunk of the tree. The head had two round black eyes, an inquisitive nose, a wide mouth with sharp teeth and whiskers like those of a cat. It seemed as big as the moon to the shy little child-larks, until it occurred to the girl that the strange creature must be a squirrel.

"You – you scared us!" she said, timidly.

"You scared *me*, at first," returned the squirrel, in a comic tone. "Dear me! how came you birds to have children's heads?"

"That isn't the way to put it," remarked Chubbins, staring back into the eyes of the squirrel. "You should ask how we children happened to have birds' bodies."

"Very well; put the conundrum that way, if you like," said the squirrel. "What is the answer?"

"We are enchanted," replied Twinkle.

"Ah. The tuxix?"

"Yes. We were caught in the forest, and she bewitched us."

"That is too bad," said their new acquaintance. "She is a very wicked old creature, for a fact, and loves to get folks into trouble. Are you going to live here?"

"Yes," answered the girl. "Policeman Bluejay gave us this nest."

"Then it's all right; for Policeman Bluejay rules the feathered tribes of this forest about as he likes. Have you seen him in full uniform yet?"

"No," they replied, "unless his feathers are his uniform."

"Well, he's too proud of his office to be satisfied with feathers, I can tell you. When some folks get a little authority they want all the world to know about it, and a bold uniform covers many a faint heart. But as I'm your nearest neighbor I'll introduce myself. My name's Wisk."

"My name is Twinkle."

"And mine's Chubbins."

"Pleased to make your acquaintance," said the squirrel, nodding. "I live in the second flat."

"How's that?" asked the boy.

"Why, the second hollow, you know. There's a 'possum living in the hollow down below, who is carrying four babies around in her pocket; and Mrs. Hootaway, the grey owl, lives in the hollow above – the one you can see far over your heads. So I'm the second flat tenant."

"I see," said Twinkle.

"Early in the morning the 'possum comes growling home to go to bed; late at night the owl hoots and keeps folks awake; but I'm very quiet and well behaved, and you'll find me a good neighbor," continued Wisk.

"I'm sure of that," said Chubbins.

As if to prove his friendship the squirrel now darted out of the hollow and sat upon a limb beside the children, holding his bushy tail straight up so that it stood above his head like a big plume in a soldier's helmet.

"Are you hungry?" asked the girl.

"Not very. I cannot get much food until the nuts are ripe, you know, and my last winter's supply was gone long ago. But I manage to find some bits to eat, here and there."

"Do you like cookies?" she asked.

"I really do not know," answered Wisk. "Where do they grow?"

"In baskets. I'll get you a piece, and you can try it." So Twinkle flew up and crept into her basket again, quickly returning with a bit of cookie in her claw. It was not much more than a crumb, but nevertheless it was all that she could carry.

The squirrel seized the morsel in his paws, examined it gravely, and then took a nibble. An instant later it was gone.

"That is very good, indeed!" he declared. "Where do these baskets of cookies grow?"

"They don't grow anywhere," replied Twinkle, with a laugh. "The baskets come from the grocery store, and my mama makes the cookies."

"Oh; they're human food, then."

"Yes; would you like some more?"

"Not just now," said Wisk. "I don't want to rob you, and it is foolish to eat more than one needs, just because the food tastes good. But if I get very hungry, perhaps I'll ask you for another bite."

"Do," said the girl. "You are welcome to what we have, as long as it lasts."

"That is very kind of you," returned the squirrel.

They sat and talked for an hour, and Wisk told them stories of the forest, and of the many queer animals and birds that lived there. It was all very interesting to the children, and they listened eagerly until they heard a rushing sound in the air that sent Wisk scurrying back into his hole.

Chapter IV

An Afternoon Reception

Twinkle and Chubbins stretched their little necks to see what was coming, and a moment later beheld one of the most gorgeous sights the forest affords – a procession of all the bright-hued birds that live among the trees or seek them for shelter.

They flew in pairs, one after the other, and at the head of the procession was their good friend Policeman Bluejay, wearing a policeman's helmet upon his head and having a policeman's club tucked underneath his left wing. The helmet was black and glossy and had a big number "1" on the front of it, and a strap that passed under the wearer's bill and held it firmly in place. The club was fastened around the policeman's wing with a cord, so that it could not get away when he was flying.

The birds were of many sizes and of various colorings. Some were much larger than the bluejay, but none seemed so proud or masterful, and all deferred meekly to the commands of the acknowledged guardian of the forest.

One by one the pretty creatures alighted upon the limbs of the tree, and the first thing they all did was to arrange their feathers properly after their rapid flight. Then the bluejay, who sat next to the child-larks, proceeded to introduce the guests he had brought to call upon the newest inhabitants of his domain.

"This is Mr. and Mrs. Robin Redbreast, one of our most aristocratic families," said he, swinging his club around in a circle until Chubbins ducked his head for fear it might hit him.

"You are welcome to our forest," chirped Robin, in a sedate and dignified tone.

"And here is Mr. Goldfinch and his charming bride," continued the policeman.

"Ah, it is a pleasure to meet you," the goldfinch murmured, eyeing the child-larks curiously, but trying to be so polite that they would not notice his staring.

"Henny Wren and Jenny Wren," proceeded the policeman.

Twinkle and Chubbins both bowed politely.

"Well, well!" croaked a raven, in a hoarse voice, "am I to wait all day while you introduce those miserable little insignificant grub-eaters?"

"Be quiet!" cried Policeman Bluejay, sternly.

"I won't," snapped the raven.

It happened so quickly that the children saw nothing before they heard the thump of the club against the raven's head.

"Caw – waw – waw – waw! Murder! Help!" screamed the big bird, and flew away from the tree as swiftly as his ragged wings would carry him.

"Let him go," said a sweet brown mocking-bird. "The rowdy is always disturbing our social gatherings, and no one will miss him if he doesn't come back."

"He is not fit for polite society," added a nuthatcher, pruning her scarlet wings complacently.

So the policeman tucked the club under his wing again and proceeded with the introductions, the pewees and the linnets being next presented to the strangers, and then the comical little chickadees, the orioles, bobolinks, thrushes, starlings and whippoorwills, the latter appearing sleepy because, they explained, they had been out late the night before.

These smaller birds all sat in rows on the limbs beside Twinkle and Chubbins; but seated upon the stouter limbs facing them were rows of bigger birds who made the child-larks nervous by the sharp glances from their round, bright eyes. Here were blackbirds, cuckoos, magpies, grosbeaks and wood-pigeons, all nearly as big and fierce-looking as Policeman Bluejay himself, and some so rugged and strong that it seemed strange they would submit to the orders of the officer of the law. But the policeman kept a sharp watch upon these birds, to see that they attempted no mischievous pranks, and they must have been afraid of him because they behaved very well after the saucy raven had left them. Even the chattering magpies tried to restrain their busy tongues, and the blackbirds indulged in no worse pranks than to suddenly spread their wings and try to push the pigeons off the branch.

Several beautiful hummingbirds were poised in the air above this gathering, their bodies being motionless but their tiny wings fluttering so swiftly that neither Twinkle nor Chubbins could see them at all.

Policeman Bluejay, having finally introduced all the company to the child-larks, began to relate the story of their adventures, telling the birds how the wicked tuxix had transformed them into the remarkable shapes they now possessed.

"For the honor of our race," he said, "we must each and every one guard these little strangers carefully, and see that they come to no harm in our forest. You must all pledge yourselves to befriend them on all occasions, and if anyone dares to break his promise he must fight with me to the death – and you know very well what that means."

"We do," said a magpie, with a shrill laugh. "You'll treat us as you did Jim Crow. Eh?"

The policeman did not notice this remark, but the other birds all looked grave and thoughtful, and began in turn to promise that they would take care to befriend the child-larks at all times. This ceremony having been completed, the birds began to converse in a more friendly and easy tone, so that Twinkle and Chubbins soon ceased to be afraid of them, and enjoyed very much their society and friendly chatter.

Chapter V

The Oriole's Story

"We are really very happy in this forest," said an oriole that sat next to Twinkle, "and we would have no fears at all did not the men with guns, who are called hunters, come here now and then to murder us. They are terribly wild and ferocious creatures, who have no hearts at all."

"Oh, they *must* have hearts," said Twinkle, "else they couldn't live. For one's heart has to beat to keep a person alive, you know."

"Perhaps it's their gizzards that beat," replied the oriole, reflectively, "for they are certainly heartless and very wicked. A cousin of mine, Susie Oriole, had a very brave and handsome husband. They built a pretty nest together and Susie laid four eggs in it that were so perfect that she was very proud of them.

"The eggs were nearly ready to hatch when a great man appeared in the forest and discovered Susie's nest. Her brave husband fought desperately to protect their home, but the cruel man shot him, and he fell to the ground dead. Even then Susie would not leave her pretty eggs, and when the man climbed the tree to get them she screamed and tried to peck out his eyes. Usually we orioles are very timid, you know; so you can well understand how terrified Susie was to fight against this giant foe. But he had a club in his hand, with which he dealt my poor cousin such a dreadful blow that she was sent whirling through the air and sank half unconscious into a bush a few yards away.

"After this the man stole the eggs from the nest, and also picked up the dead body of Susie's husband and carried it away with him. Susie recovered somewhat from the blow she had received, and when she saw her eggs and her poor dead husband being taken away, she managed to flutter along after the man and followed him until he came to the edge of the forest. There he had a horse tied to a tree, and he mounted upon the beast's back and rode away through the open country. Susie followed him, just far enough away to keep the man in sight, without being noticed herself.

"By and bye he came to a big house, which he entered, closing the door behind him. Susie flew into a tree beside the house and waited sorrowfully but in patience for a chance to find her precious ones again.

"The days passed drearily away, one after another, but in about a week my cousin noticed that one of the windows of the house had been left open. So she boldly left her tree and flew in at the window, and luckily none of the people who lived in the house happened to be in the room.

"Imagine Susie's surprise when she saw around the sides of the room many birds sitting silently upon limbs cut from trees, and among them her own husband, as proud and beautiful as he had ever been before the cruel man had killed him! She quickly flew to the limb and perched beside her loved one.

"'Oh, my darling!' she cried, 'how glad I am to have found you again, and to see you alive and well when I had mourned you as dead. Come with me at once, and we will return to our old home in the forest.'

"But the bird remained motionless and made no reply to her loving words. She thrust her bill beside his and tried to kiss him, but he did not respond to the caress and his body was stiff and cold.

"Then Susie uttered a cry of grief, and understood the truth. Her husband was indeed dead, but had been stuffed and mounted upon the limb to appear as he had in life. Small wires had been pushed through his legs to make his poor body stand up straight, and to Susie's horror she discovered that his eyes were only bits of glass! All the other birds in the room were stuffed in the same way. They looked as if they were alive, at the first glance; but each body was cold and every voice mute. They were mere mockeries of the beautiful birds that this heartless and cruel man had deprived of their joyous lives.

"Susie's loving heart was nearly bursting with pain as she slowly fluttered toward the open window by which she had entered. But on her way a new anguish overtook her, for she noticed a big glass case against the wall in which were arranged clusters of eggs stolen from birds of almost every kind. Yes; there were her own lovely eggs, scarcely an inch from her face, but separated from her by a stout glass that could not be broken, although she madly dashed her body against it again and again.

"Finally, realizing her helplessness, poor Susie left the room by the open window and flew back to the forest, where she told us all the terrible thing she had seen. No one was able to comfort her, for her loving heart was broken; and after that she would often fly away to the house to peer through the window at her eggs and her beautiful husband.

"One day she did not return, and after waiting for her nearly two weeks we sent the bluejay to see what had become of her. Our policeman found the house, and also found the window of the room open.

"He boldly entered, and discovered Susie and her husband sitting side by side upon the dried limb, their bodies both stiff and dead. The man had caught the poor wife at last, and the lovers were reunited in death.

"Also Policeman Bluejay found his grandfather's mummy in this room, and the stuffed mummies of many other friends he had known in the forest. So he was very sorrowful when he returned to us, and from that time we have feared the heartless men more than ever."

"It's a sad story," sighed Twinkle, "and I've no doubt it is a true one. But all men are not so bad, I'm sure."

"All men who enter the forest are," answered the oriole, positively. "For they only come here to murder and destroy those who are helpless before their power, but have never harmed them in the least. If God loves the birds, as I am sure He does, why do you suppose He made their ferocious enemies, the men?"

Twinkle did not reply, but she felt a little ashamed.

Chapter VI

A Merry Adventure

"Talking about men," said the cuckoo, in a harsh but not very unpleasant voice, "reminds me of a funny adventure I once had myself. I was sitting in my nest one day, at the time when I was quite young, when suddenly a man appeared before me. You must know that this nest, which was rather carelessly built by my mother, was in a thick evergreen tree, and not very high from the ground; so that I found the man's eyes staring squarely into my own.

"Most of you, my dears, have seen men; but this was the strangest sort of man you can imagine. There was white hair upon his face, so long that it hung down to his middle, and over his eyes were round plates of glass that glittered very curiously. I was so astonished at seeing the queer creature that I sat still and stared, and this was my undoing. For suddenly there came a rapid 'whish!' through the air, and a network of cords fell all around and over me. Then, indeed, I spread my wings and attempted to fly; but it was too late. I struggled in the net without avail, and soon gave up the conflict in breathless despair.

"My captor did not intend to kill me, however. Instead, he tried to soothe my fright, and carried me very gently for many, many miles, until we came to a village of houses. Here, at the very top of a high house, the man lived in one little room. It was all littered with tools and bits of wood, and on a broad shelf were several queer things that went 'tick-tock! tick-tock!' every minute. I was thrust, gently enough, into a wooden cage, where I lay upon the bottom more dead than alive because the ticking things at first scared me dreadfully and I was in constant terror lest I should be tortured or killed. But the glass-eyed old man brought me dainty things to eat, and plenty of fresh water to relieve my thirst, and by the next day my heart had stopped going pitty-pat and I was calm enough to stand up in my cage and look around me.

"My white-whiskered captor sat at a bench with his coat off and his bald head bare, while he worked away busily putting little wheels and springs together, and fitting them into a case of wood. When one of them was finished it would sing 'tick-tock! tick-tock!' just like the other queer things on the shelf, and this constant ticking so interested me that I raised my head and called:

"'Cuck-oo! cuck-oo!'"

"'That's it!' cried the old man, delightedly. 'That's what I wanted to hear. It's the real cuckoo at last, and not a bit like those cheap imitations.'

"I didn't understand at first what he meant, but he worked at his bench all day, and finally brought to my cage a bird made out of wood, that was carved and painted to look just as I was. It seemed so natural that I flapped my wings and called 'cuck-oo' to it, and the man pressed a little bellows at the bottom of the bird and made it say 'cuck-oo!' in return. But that cry was so false and unreal that I just shouted with laughter, and the glass-eyed old man shook his head sadly and said: 'That will never do. That will never do in the world.'

"So all the next day he worked hard trying to make his wooden bird say 'cuck-oo!' in the proper way; and at last it really spoke quite naturally, so that it startled even me when I heard it. This seemed to please my captor very much; so he put it inside one of the ticking things on the shelf, and by-and-by a door opened and the wooden bird jumped out and cried 'Cuck-oo! Cuck-oo! Cuck-oo!' and then jumped back again and the door closed with a snap.

"'Bravo!' cried old white-hair; but I was rather annoyed, for I thought the wooden bird was impudent in trying to ape the ways of live cuckoos. I shouted back a challenge to it, but there was no reply. An hour later, and every hour, it repeated the performance, but jumped behind the door when I offered to fight it.

"The next day the man was absent from the room, and I had nothing to eat. So I became angry and uneasy. I scratched away at the wooden bars of my cage and tried to twist them with my beak, and at last one of them, to my great joy, came loose, and I was able to squeeze myself out of the cage.

"But then I was no better off than before, because the windows and the door of the room were fast shut. I grew more cross and ill-tempered than before, when I discovered this, and to add to my annoyance that miserable wooden bird would every once in awhile jump out and yell 'Cuck-oo!' and then bounce back into its house again, without daring to argue with me.

"This at last made me frantic with rage, and I resolved to be revenged. The next time the wooden bird made its appearance I new upon it in a flash and knocked it off the little platform before it had uttered its cry more than twice. It fell upon the floor and broke one of its wings; but in an instant I dashed myself upon it and bit and scratched the impudent thing until there was not a bit of paint left upon it. Its head came off, too, and so did its legs and the other wing, and before I was done with it no one ever would have known it was once a clever imitation of myself. Finding that I was victorious I cried 'Cuck-oo!' in triumph, and just then the little door of the ticking thing opened and the platform where the wooden bird had stood came out of it and remained for a time motionless. I quickly flew up and perched upon it, and shouted 'Cuck-oo!' again, in great glee. As I did so, to my amazement the platform on which I stood leaped backward, carrying me with it, and the next instant the door closed with a snap and I found myself in darkness.

"Wildly I fluttered my wings; but it was of no use. I was in a prison much worse than the cage, and so small that I could hardly turn around in it. I was about to die of terror and despair when I chanced to remember that at certain times the door would open to push out the bird and allow it to say 'Cuck-oo!' before it shut again. So, the next time it opened in this way, I would be able to make my escape.

"Very patiently I waited in the dark little hole, listening to the steady 'tick-tock!' of the machinery behind me and trying not to be nervous. After awhile I heard the old man come into the room and exclaim sorrowfully because his captive cuckoo had escaped from its cage. He could not imagine what had become of me, and I kept still and laughed to myself to think how I would presently surprise him.

"It seemed an age before I finally heard the click that opened the door in front of me. Then the platform on which I sat sprang out, and I fluttered my wings and yelled 'Cuck-oo! Cuck-oo!' as loud as I could. The old man was standing right in front of me, his mouth wide open with astonishment at the wonderfully natural performance of his wooden bird, as he thought me. He shouted 'Bravo!' again, and clapped his hands; and at that I flew straight into his face, and clawed his white hair with all my might, and screamed as loud as I could.

"He screamed, too, being taken by surprise, and tumbled over backward so that he sat down upon the floor with a loud bump. I flew to the work-bench, and then the truth dawned upon him that I was not the wooden bird but the real one.

"'Good gracious!' said he, 'I've left the window open. The rascal will escape!'

"I glanced at the window and saw that it was indeed wide open. The sight filled me with triumphant joy. Before the old man could get upon his feet and reach the window I had perched upon the sill, and with one parting cry of 'Cuck-oo!' I spread my wings and flew straight into the air.

"Well, I never went back to enquire if he enjoyed the trick I had played upon him, but I've laughed many a time when I thought of the old fellow's comic expression when a real cuckoo instead of a painted one flew out of his ticking machine."

As the cuckoo ended his tale the other birds joined in a chorus of shrill laughter; but Chubbins said to them, gravely:

"He was a smart man, though, to make a cuckoo-clock. I saw one myself, one time, and it was a wonderful thing. The cuckoo told what time it was every hour."

"Was it made of wood?" asked the bluejay.

"I don't know that," replied the boy-lark; "but of course it wasn't a real bird."

"It only shows," remarked the bobolink, "how greatly those humans admire us birds. They make pictures of us, and love to keep us in cages so they can hear us sing, and they even wear us in their bonnets after we are dead."

"I think that is a dreadful thing," said the goldfinch, with a shudder. "But it only proves that men are our greatest enemies."

"Don't forget the women," said Twinkle. "It's the women that wear birds in their hats."

"Mankind," said Robin Redbreast, gravely, "is the most destructive and bloodthirsty of all the brute creation. They not only kill for food, but through vanity and a desire for personal adornment. I have even heard it said that they kill for amusement, being unable to restrain their murderous desires. In this they are more cruel than the serpents."

"There is some excuse for the poor things," observed the bluejay, "for nature created them dependent upon the animals and birds and fishes. Having neither fur nor feathers to protect their poor skinny bodies, they wear clothing made of the fleece of sheep, and skins of seals and beavers and otters and even the humble muskrats. They cover their feet and their hands with skins of beasts; they sleep upon the feathers of birds; their food is the flesh of beasts and birds and fishes. No created thing is so dependent upon others as man; therefore he is the greatest destroyer in the world. But he is not alone in his murderous, despoiling instinct. While you rail at man, my friends, do not forget that birds are themselves the greatest enemies of birds."

"Nonsense!" cried the magpie, indignantly.

"Perhaps the less you say about this matter the better," declared the bluejay, swinging his club in a suggestive manner, and looking sharply at the magpie.

"It's a slander," said the blackbird. "I'm sure you can't accuse *me* of injuring birds in any way."

"If you are all innocent, why are we obliged to have a policeman?" enquired the little wren, in a nervous voice.

"Tell me," said Twinkle, appealing to the bluejay; "are the big birds really naughty to the little ones?"

"Why, it is the same with us as it is with men," replied the policeman. "There are good ones and bad ones among us, and the bad ones have to be watched. Men destroy us wantonly; other animals and the sly serpents prey upon us and our eggs for food; but these are open enemies, and we know how we may best avoid them. Our most dangerous foes are those bandits of our own race who, instead of protecting their brethren, steal our eggs and murder our young. They are not always the biggest birds, by any means, that do these things. The crow family is known to be treacherous, and the shrike is rightly called the 'butcher-bird,' but there are many others that we have reason to suspect feed upon their own race."

"How dreadful!" exclaimed the girl-lark.

The birds all seemed restless and uneasy at this conversation, and looked upon one another with suspicious glances. But the bluejay soothed them by saying:

"After all, I suppose we imagine more evil than really exists, and sometimes accuse our neighbors wrongfully. But the mother birds know how often their nests have been robbed in their absence, and if they suspect some neighbor of the crime instead of a prowling animal it is but natural, since many birds cannot be trusted. There are laws in the forest, of course; but the guilty ones are often able to escape. I'll tell you of a little tragedy that happened only last week, which will prove how apt we are to be mistaken."

Chapter VII

The Bluejay's Story

"There is no more faithful mother in the forest than the blue titmouse, which is a cousin to the chickadee," continued the policeman, "and this spring Tom Titmouse and his wife Nancy set up housekeeping in a little hollow in an elm tree about half a mile north of this spot. Of course, the first thing Nancy did was to lay six beautiful eggs – white with brown spots all over them – in the nest. Tom was as proud of these eggs as was Nancy, and as the nest was hidden in a safe place they flew away together to hunt for caterpillars, and had no thought of danger. But on their return an hour later what was their sorrow to find the nest empty, and every pretty egg gone. On the ground underneath the tree were scattered a few bits of shell; but the robber was nowhere to be seen.

"Tom Titmouse was very indignant at this dreadful crime, and came to me at once to complain of the matter; but of course I had no idea who had done the deed. I questioned all the birds who have ever been known to slyly steal eggs, and everyone denied the robbery. So Nancy Titmouse saw she must lay more eggs, and before long had another six speckled beauties in the bottom of her nest.

"They were more careful now about leaving home; but the danger seemed past. One bright, sunny morning they ventured to fly to the brook to drink and bathe themselves, and on their return found their home despoiled for a second time. Not an egg was left to them out of the six, and while Nancy wept and wailed Tom looked sharply around him and saw a solitary shrike sitting on a limb not far away."

"What's a shrike?" asked Chubbins.

"It is a bird that looks a good deal like that mocking-bird sitting next you; but it bears a bad character in the forest and has earned the vile name of 'butcher-bird.' I admit that I am always obliged to keep an eye upon the shrike, for I expect it to get into mischief at any time. Well, Tom Titmouse naturally thought the shrike had eaten Nancy's eggs, so he came to me and ordered me to arrest the robber. But the shrike pleaded his innocence, and I had no proof against him.

"Again Nancy, with true motherly courage and perseverance, laid her eggs in the nest; and now they were never left alone for a single minute. Either she or Tom was always at home, and for my part I watched the shrike carefully and found he did not fly near the nest of the titmice at all.

"The result of our care was that one fine day the eggs hatched out, and six skinny little titmice, with big heads and small bodies, were nestling against Nancy's breast. The mother thought they were beautiful, you may be sure, and many birds gathered around to congratulate her and Tom, and the brown thrush sang a splendid song of welcome to the little ones.

"When the children got a little stronger it did not seem necessary to guard the nest so closely, and the six appetites required a good many insects and butterfly-eggs to satisfy them. So Tom and Nancy both flew away to search for food, and when they came back they found, to their horror, that their six little ones had been stolen, and the nest was bare and cold. Nancy nearly fainted with sorrow, and her cries were pitiful and heart-rending; but Tom Titmouse was dreadfully angry, and came to me demanding vengeance.

"'If you are any good at all as a policeman,' said he, 'you will discover and punish the murderer of my babies.'

"So I looked all around and finally discovered, not far from the nest of the titmice, four of their children, all dead and each one impaled upon the thorn of a bush that grew close to the ground. Then I decided it was indeed the shrike, for he has a habit of doing just this thing; killing more than he can eat and sticking the rest of his murdered victims on thorns until he finds time to come back and devour them.

"I was also angry, by that time; so I flew to the shrike's nest and found him all scratched and torn and his feathers plucked in many places.

"'What has happened to you?' I asked.

"'I had a fight with a weasel last night,' answered the shrike, 'and both of us are rather used up, today.'

"'Still,' said I, sternly, 'you had strength enough to kill the six little titmice, and to eat two of them.'

"'I never did,' said he, earnestly; 'my wings are too stiff to fly.'

"'Do not lie about it, I beg of you,' said I; 'for we have found four of the dead titmice stuck on the thorns of a bush, and your people have been known to do such things before.'

"At this the shrike looked worried.

"'Really,' said he, 'I cannot understand it. But I assure you I am innocent.'

"Nevertheless, I arrested him, and made him fly with me to the Judgment Tree, where all the birds had congregated. He was really stiff and sore, and I could see it hurt him to fly; but my duty was plain. We selected a jury of twelve birds, and Judge Bullfinch took his seat on a bough, and then the trial began.

"Tom Titmouse accused the shrike of murder, and so did Nancy, who had nearly cried her eyes out. I also gave my evidence. But the prisoner insisted strongly that he was innocent, and claimed he had not left his nest since his fight with the weasel, and so was guiltless of the crime.

"But no one had any sympathy for him, or believed what he said; for it is often the case that when one has earned a bad character he is thought capable of any wickedness. So the jury declared him guilty, and the judge condemned him to die at sundown. We were all to fall upon the prisoner together, and tear him into bits with bill and claw; but while we waited for the sun to sink Will Sparrow flew up to the Judgment Tree and said:

"'Hello! What's going on here?'

"'We are just about to execute a criminal,' replied the judge.

"'What has he been doing?' asked Will, eyeing the shrike curiously.

"'He killed the titmice children this morning, and ate two of them, and stuck the other four upon a thorn bush,' explained the judge.

"'Oh, no; the shrike did not do that!' cried Will Sparrow. 'I saw the crime committed with my own eyes, and it was the cunning weasel – the one that lives in the pine stump – that did the dreadful murder.'

"At this all the birds set up an excited chatter, and the shrike again screamed that he was innocent. So the judge said, gravely: 'Will Sparrow always speaks the truth. Release the prisoner, for we have misjudged him. We must exact our vengeance upon the weasel.'

"So we all flew swiftly to the pine stump, which we knew well, and when we arrived we found the weasel sitting at the edge of his hole and laughing at us.

"'That is the very weasel I fought with,' said the shrike. 'You can see where I tore the fur from his head and back with my sharp beak.'

"'So you did,' answered the weasel; 'and in return I killed the little tomtits.'

"'Did you stick them on the thorns?' asked Judge Bullfinch.

"'Yes,' said the weasel. 'I hoped you would accuse the shrike of the murder, and kill him to satisfy my vengeance.'

"'We nearly fell into the trap,' returned the judge; 'but Will Sparrow saw your act and reported it just in time to save the shrike's life. But tell me, did you also eat Nancy Titmouse's eggs?'

"'Of course,' confessed the weasel, 'and they were very good, indeed.'

"Hearing this, Tom Titmouse became so excited that he made a furious dash at the weasel, who slipped within his hole and escaped.

"'I condemn you to death!' cried the judge.

"'That's all right,' answered the weasel, sticking just the tip of his nose out of the hole. 'But you've got to catch me before you can kill me. Run home, my pretty birds. You're no match for a weasel!'

"Then he was gone from sight, and we knew he was hidden safely in the stump, where we could not follow him, for the weasel's body is slim and slender. But I have not lived in the forest all my life without learning something, and I whispered a plan to Judge Bullfinch that met with his approval. He sent messengers at once for the ivory-billed woodpeckers, and soon four of those big birds appeared and agreed to help us. They began tearing away at the stump with their strong beaks, and the splinters flew in every direction. It was not yet dark when the cunning weasel was dragged from his hole and was at the mercy of the birds he had so cruelly offended. We fell upon him in a flash, and he was dead almost instantly."

"What became of the shrike?" asked Twinkle.

"He left the forest the next day," answered Policeman Bluejay. "For although he was innocent of this crime, he was still a butcher-bird, and he knew our people had no confidence in him."

"It was lucky Will Sparrow came in time," said the girl-lark. "But all these stories must have made you hungry, so I'd like to invite my guests to have some refreshments."

The birds seemed much surprised by this invitation, and even Policeman Bluejay wondered what she was going to do. But Twinkle whispered to Chubbins, and both the bird-children flew into their basket and returned with their claws full of cookie. They repeated the journey many times, distributing bits of the rare food to all of the birds who had visited them, and each one ate the morsel eagerly and declared that it was very good.

"Now," said the policeman, when the feast was over, "let us all go to the brook and have a drink of its clear, sweet water."

So they flew away, a large and merry band of all sizes and colors; and the child-larks joined them, skimming the air as lightly and joyously as any of their new friends. It did not take them long to reach a sparkling brook that wound its way through the forest, and all the feathered people drank their fill standing upon the low bank or upon stones that rose above the level of the water.

At first the children were afraid they might fall into the brook; but presently they gained courage, and when they saw the thrush and bullfinch plunge in and bathe themselves in the cool water Chubbins decided to follow their example, and afterward Twinkle also joined them.

The birds now bade the child-larks good-bye and promised to call upon them again, and soon all had flown away except the bluejay, who said he would see Twinkle and Chubbins safe home again, so that they would not get lost.

They thanked him for this kindness, and when they had once more settled upon the limb beside their nest the bluejay also bade them good night and darted away for one last look through the forest to see that all was orderly for the night.

Chapter VIII

Mrs. Hootaway

As the child-larks sat side by side upon their limb, with the soft grey nest near at hand, the twilight fell and a shadow began to grow and deepen throughout the forest.

"Twink," said Chubbins, gravely, "how do you like it?"

"Well," replied the girl, "it isn't so bad in the daytime, but it's worse at night. That bunch of grass mixed up with the stems of leaves, that they call a nest, isn't much like my pretty white bed at home, Chubbins."

"Nor mine," he agreed. "And, Twink, how ever can we say our prayers when we haven't any hands to hold up together?"

"Prayers, Chub," said the girl, "are more in our hearts than in our hands. It isn't what we *do* that counts; it's what we feel. But the most that bothers me is what the folks at home will think, when we don't come back."

"They'll hunt for us," Chubbins suggested; "and they may come under this tree, and call to us."

"If they do," said Twinkle, "we'll fly right down to them."

"I advise you not to fly much, in the night," said a cheery voice beside them, and Wisk the squirrel stuck his head out of the hollow where he lived. "You've had quite a party here today," he continued, "and they behaved pretty well while the policeman was around. But some of them might not be so friendly if you met them alone."

"Would any bird hurt us?" asked the girl, in surprise.

"Why, I've seen a magpie meet a thrush, and fly away alone," replied Wisk. "And the wrens and chickadees avoid the cuckoo as much as possible, because they are fond of being alive. But the policeman keeps the big birds all in order when he is around, and he makes them all afraid to disobey the laws. He's a wonderful fellow, that Policeman Bluejay, and even we squirrels are glad he is in the forest."

"Why?" asked Chubbins.

"Well, we also fear some of the birds," answered Wisk. "The lady in the third flat, for instance, Mrs. Hootaway, is said to like a squirrel for a midnight meal now and then, when mice and beetles are scarce. It is almost her hour for wakening, so I must be careful to keep near home."

"Tut – tut – tut!" cried a harsh voice from above. "What scandal is this you are talking, Mr. Wisk?"

The squirrel was gone in a flash; but a moment later he put out his head again and turned one bright eye toward the upper part of the tree. There, on a perch outside her hollow, sat the grey owl, pruning her feathers. It was nearly dark by this time, and through the dusk Mrs. Hootaway's yellow eyes could be seen gleaming bright and wide open.

"What nonsense are you putting into the heads of these little innocents?" continued the owl, in a scolding tone.

"No nonsense at all," said Wisk, in reply. "The child-larks are safe enough from you, because they are under the protection of Policeman Bluejay, and he would have a fine revenge if you dared to hurt them. But my case is different. The laws of the birds do not protect squirrels, and when you're abroad, my dear Mrs. Hootaway, I prefer to remain snugly at home."

"To be sure," remarked the owl, with a laugh. "You are timid and suspicious by nature, my dear Wisk, and you forget that although I have known you for a long time I have never yet eaten you."

"That is my fault, and not yours," retorted the squirrel.

"Well, I'm not after you tonight, neighbor, nor after birds, either. I know where there are seven fat mice to be had, and until they are all gone you may cease to worry."

"I'm glad to hear that," replied Wisk. "I wish there were seven hundred mice to feed your appetite. But I'm not going to run into danger recklessly, nevertheless, and it is my bedtime. So good night, Mrs. Hootaway; and good night, little child-larks." The owl did not reply, but Twinkle and Chubbins called good night to the friendly squirrel, and then they hopped into their nest and cuddled down close together.

The moon was now rising over the trees and flooding the gloom of the forest with its subdued silver radiance. The children were not sleepy; their new life was too strange and wonderful for them to be able to close their eyes at once. So they were rather pleased when the grey owl settled on the branch beside their nest and began to talk to them.

"I'm used to slanders, my dears," she said, in a pleasanter tone than she had used before, "so I don't mind much what neighbor Wisk says to me. But I do not wish you to think ill of the owl family, and so I must assure you that we are as gentle and kindly as any feathered creatures in the forest – not excepting the Birds of Paradise."

"I am sure of that," replied Twinkle, earnestly. "You are too soft and fluffy and pretty to be bad."

"It isn't the prettiness," said the grey owl, evidently pleased by the compliment. "It is the nature of owls to be kind and sympathetic. Those who do not know us very well say harsh things about us, because we fly in the night, when most other birds are asleep, and sleep in the daytime when most other birds are awake."

"Why do you do that?" asked Chubbins.

"Because the strong light hurts our eyes. But, although we are abroad in the night, we seek only our natural prey, and obey the Great Law of the forest more than some others do."

"What is the Great Law?" enquired Twinkle, curiously.

"Love. It is the moral law that is above all laws made by living creatures. The whole forest is ruled by love more than it is by fear. You may think this is strange when you remember that some animals eat birds, and some birds eat animals, and the dreadful creeping things eat us both; but nevertheless we are so close to Nature here that love and tenderness for our kind influences us even more than it does mankind – the careless and unthinking race from which you came. The residents of the forest are good parents, helpful neighbors, and faithful friends. What better than this could be said of us?"

"Nothing, I'm sure, if it is true," replied the girl.

"Over in the Land of Paradise," continued the owl, thoughtfully, "the birds are not obliged to take life in order to live themselves; so they call us savage and fierce. But I believe our natures are as kindly as those of the Birds of Paradise."

"Where is this Land of Paradise you speak of?" asked Twinkle.

"Directly in the center of our forest. It is a magical spot, protected from intrusion not by any wall or barred gates, but by a strong wind that blows all birds away from that magnificent country except the Birds of Paradise themselves. There is a legend that man once lived there, but for some unknown crime was driven away. But the birds have always been allowed to inhabit the place because they did no harm."

"I'd like to see it," said Chubbins.

"So would I," confessed the grey owl, with a sigh; "but there is no use of my attempting to get into the Paradise of Birds, because the wind would blow me back. But now it is getting quite dark, and I must be off to seek my food. Mrs. 'Possum and I have agreed to hunt together, tonight."

"Who is Mrs. 'Possum?" the girl asked.

"An animal living in the lowest hollow of this tree," answered the owl. "She is a good-natured creature, and hunts by night, as I do. She is slow, but, being near the ground, she can spy a mouse much quicker than I can, and then she calls to me to catch it. So between us we get plenty of game and are helpful to each other. The only drawback is that Mrs. 'Possum has four children, which she carries in her pouch wherever she goes, and they have to be fed as well as their mother. So the 'possums have five mouths to my one, and it keeps us busy to supply them all."

"It's very kind of you to help her," remarked Twinkle.

"Oh, she helps me, too," returned the owl, cheerfully. "But now good night, my dears. You will probably be sound asleep when I get home again."

Off flew Mrs. Hootaway with these words, and her wings moved so noiselessly that she seemed to fade away into the darkness like a ghost.

The child-larks sat looking at the silver moon for a time; but presently Twinkle's eyelids drooped and she fell fast asleep, and Chubbins was not long in following her example.

Chapter IX

The Destroyers

A loud shouting and a bang that echoed like a clap of thunder through the forest awoke the bird-children from their dreams.

Opening their eyes with a start they saw that the grey dawn was breaking and a sort of morning twilight made all objects in the forest distinct, yet not so brilliant as the approaching daylight would. Shadows still lay among the bushes and the thickest branches; but between the trees the spaces were clearly visible.

The children, rudely awakened by the riot of noise in their ears, could distinguish the barking of dogs, the shouts of men calling to the brutes, and the scream of an animal in deep distress. Immediately after, there was a whirl overhead and the grey owl settled on the limb beside their nest.

"They've got her!" she exclaimed, in a trembling, terrified voice. "The men have shot Mrs. 'Possum dead, and the dogs are now tearing her four babies limb from limb!"

"Where are they?" whispered Twinkle, her little heart beating as violently as if the dread destroyers had always been her mortal enemies.

"Just below us. Isn't it dreadful? We had such a nice night together, and Mrs. 'Possum was so sweet and loving in caring for her little ones and feeding them! And, just as we were nearly home again, the dogs sprang upon my friend and the men shot her dead. We had not even suspected, until then, that our foes were in the forest."

Twinkle and Chubbins craned their necks over the edge of the nest and looked down. On the ground stood a man and a boy, and two great dogs were growling fiercely and tearing some bloody, revolting object with their cruel jaws.

"Look out!" cried the voice of Wisk, the squirrel. "He's aiming at you – look out!"

They ducked their heads again, just as the gun roared and flamed fire beneath them.

"Oh-h-h!" wailed Mrs. Hootaway, fluttering violently beside them. "They struck me that time – the bullet is in my heart. Good-bye, my dears. Remember that – all – is love; all is – love!"

Her voice died away to a whisper, and she toppled from the limb. Twinkle and Chubbins tried to save their dying friend from falling, but the grey owl was so much bigger than they that they could not support the weight of her body. Slowly she sank to the ground and fell upon the earth with a dull sound that was dreadful to hear.

Instantly Twinkle darted from the nest and swooped downward, alighting on the ground beside the owl's quivering body. A big dog came bounding toward her. The man was reloading his gun, a few paces away.

"Call off your dog!" shouted Twinkle, wildly excited. "How dare you shoot the poor, harmless birds? Call off your dog, I say!"

But, even as she spoke, the words sounded in her own ears strange and unnatural, and more like the chirping of a bird than the language of men. The hunter either did not hear her or he did not understand her, and the dog snarled and bared its wicked teeth as it sprang greedily upon the child-lark.

Twinkle was too terrified to move. She glared upon the approaching monster helplessly, and it had almost reached her when a black object fell from the skies with the swiftness of a lightning streak and struck the dog's back, tearing the flesh with its powerful talons and driving a stout, merciless beak straight through the skull of the savage brute.

The dog, already dead, straightened out and twitched convulsively. The man shouted angrily and sprang upon the huge bird that had slain his pet, at the same time swinging his gun like a club.

"Quick!" said the eagle to Twinkle, "mount with me as swiftly as you can."

With the words he rose into the air and Twinkle darted after him, while Chubbins, seeing their flight from his nest, joined them just in time to escape a shot from the boy's deadly gun.

The inquisitive squirrel, however, had stuck his head out to see what was happening, and one of the leaden bullets buried itself in his breast. Chubbins saw him fall back into his hollow and heard his agonized scream; but he could not stay to help his poor friend. An instant later he had joined the eagle and Twinkle, and was flying as hard and swift as his wonderful lark wings could carry him up, up into the blue sky.

The sunshine touched them now, while below the tragic forest still lay buried in gloom.

"We are quite safe here, for I am sure no shot from a gun could reach us," said the eagle. "So let us rest upon our wings for a while. How lucky it was that I happened to be around in time to rescue you, my little friends."

"I am very grateful, indeed," answered Twinkle, holding her wings outstretched so that she floated lightly in the air beside her rescuer. "If you had been an instant later, the dog would have killed me."

"Very true," returned the eagle. "I saw your danger while I was in the air, and determined to act quickly, although I might myself have been shot by the man had his gun been loaded. But I have noticed that a bold action is often successful because it causes surprise, and the foe does not know what to do."

"I'm 'shamed of those people," said Chubbins, indignantly. "What right had they to come to the forest and kill the pretty owl, and the dear little squirrel, and the poor mama 'possum and her babies?"

"They had the right of power," said the eagle, calmly. "It would be a beautiful world were there no destroyers of life in it; but the earth and air and water would then soon become so crowded that there would not be room for them all to exist. Don't blame the men."

"But they are cruel," said Twinkle, "and kill innocent, harmless birds and animals, instead of the wicked ones that could be better spared."

"Cruelty is man's nature," answered the eagle. "Of all created things, men, tigers and snakes are known to be the most cruel. From them we expect no mercy. But now, what shall be our next movement? I suppose it will be best for you to keep away from the forest until the men are gone. Would you like to visit my home, and meet my wife and children?"

"Yes, indeed!" cried Twinkle; "if you will be kind enough to let us."

"It will be a great pleasure to me," said the eagle. "Follow me closely, please."

He began flying again, and they kept at his side. By and by they noticed a bright, rosy glow coming from a portion of the forest beneath them.

"What is that?" asked Chubbins.

"It is the place called the Paradise of Birds," answered their conductor. "It is said to be the most beautiful place in all the world, but no one except the Birds of Paradise are allowed to live there. Those favored birds sometimes enter our part of the forest, but we are never allowed to enter theirs."

"I'd like to see that place," said Twinkle.

"Well, you two child-larks are different from all other birds," remarked the eagle, "and for that reason perhaps you would be allowed to visit the paradise that is forbidden the rest of us. If ever I meet one of the beautiful birds that live there, I will ask it to grant you the privilege."

"Do!" said Twinkle and Chubbins, in one eager breath. They flew for a long time, high in the air, but neither of the bird-children seemed to tire in the least. They could not go quite as fast as the eagle, however, who moderated his speed so that they could keep up with him.

Chapter X

In the Eagle's Nest

Gradually the forest passed out of sight and only bleak, rugged mountains were below them. One peak rose higher than the others, and faced the sea, and to this point the great eagle directed their flight.

On a crag that jutted out from the mountain was the eagle's nest, made of rude sticks of wood gathered from the forest. Sitting beside the nest was Mrs. Eagle, larger and more pompous even than her husband, while squatting upon the edge of the nest were two half-grown eaglets with enormous claws and heads, but rather skinny bodies that were covered with loose and ragged feathers. Neither the nest nor the eaglets appeared to be very clean, and a disagreeable smell hung over the place.

"This is funny," said Mrs. Eagle, looking at the child-larks with surprise. "Usually you kill your game before you bring it home, Jonathan; but today it seems our dinner has flown to us willingly."

"They're for us!" cried one of the eaglets, making a quick dash to seize Twinkle, who darted out of his reach.

"One for each of us!" screamed the other eaglet, rushing at Chubbins.

"Peace – be quiet!" said the eagle, sternly. "Cannot you tell friends from food, you foolish youngsters? These are two little friends of mine whom I have invited to visit us; so you must treat them in a civil manner."

"Why not eat them?" asked one of the eaglets, looking at the child-larks with hungry eyes.

"Because I forbid you. They are my guests, and must be protected and well treated. And even if this were not so, the larks are too small to satisfy your hunger, you little gluttons."

"Jonathan," said Mrs. Eagle, coldly, "do not reproach our offspring for their hunger. We sent you out this morning to procure a supply of food, and we expected you to bring us home something good to eat, instead of these useless little creatures."

The eagle seemed annoyed at being scolded in this manner.

"I had an adventure in the forest," he said, "and came near being shot and killed by a man. That is the reason I came home so soon."

Twinkle and Chubbins were standing together at the edge of the crag when one of the eaglets suddenly spread out his wide, stiff wings and pushed them over the precipice. They recovered themselves before they had fallen far, and flew to the ledge again just in time to see the father eagle cuff his naughty son very soundly. But the mother only laughed in her harsh voice and said:

"It is so early in the day, Jonathan, that I advise you to go again in search of food. Our sweet darlings will not be comforted until they have eaten."

"Very well," answered the eagle. "I am sorry you cannot treat my guests more politely, for they are all unaccustomed to such rudeness. But I see that it will be better for me to take them away with me at once."

"Do," said Mrs. Eagle; and the eaglets cried: "Better let us eat 'em, daddy. They are not very big, but they're better than no breakfast at all."

"You're dis'greeable things!" said Twinkle, indignantly; "and I don't like you a bit. So *there!*"

"Come on, Twink," said Chubbins. "Let's go away."

"I will take you back to the forest," the eagle declared, and at once rose into the air. Twinkle and Chubbins followed him, and soon the nest on the crag was left far behind and they could no longer hear the hoot of the savage young ones.

For a time the eagle flew in silence. Then he said:

"You must forgive my family for not being more hospitable. You must know that they live a very lonely life, and have no society because every living thing fears them. But I go abroad more and see more of the world, so I know very well how guests ought to be treated."

"You have been very kind to us, Mr. Eagle," replied the girl-lark, "and you saved my life when the dog would have killed me. I don't blame you any for what your family did. My mama says lots of people show off better abroad than they do at home, and that's your case exactly. If I were you I wouldn't take anymore visitors to my nest."

"I do not intend to," answered the eagle. "But I am glad that you think well of me personally, if you do not of my family, and I assure you it has been a real pleasure to me to assist you. Were you like ordinary birds, you would be beneath my notice; but I am wise enough to understand that you are very unusual and wonderful little creatures, and if at any time I can serve you further, you have but to call me, and I will do what I can for you."

"Thank you very much," replied Twinkle, who realized that the great bird had acted more gently toward them than it is the nature of his wild race to do.

They had just reached the edge of the forest again when they saw a bird approaching them at a great speed, and soon it came near enough for them to see that it was Policeman Bluejay. He wore his official helmet and carried his club, and as soon as he came beside them he said:

"Thank goodness I've found you at last. I've been hunting for you an hour, and began to fear you had met with some misfortune."

"We've been with the eagle," said the girl. "He saved our lives and carried us away from where the dreadful men were."

"We have had sad doings in the forest today – very sad, indeed," declared the bluejay, in a grave voice. "The hunters did even more damage than usual. They killed Jolly Joe, the brown bear, and Sam Fox, and Mrs. 'Possum and her babies, and Wisk the squirrel; so that the animals are all in mourning for their friends. But our birds suffered greatly, also. Mrs. Hootaway is dead, and three pigeons belonging to a highly respected family; but the saddest of all is the murder of Mr. and Mrs. Goldfinch, both of whom were killed by the same shot. You may remember, my dears, that they were at your reception yesterday, and as gay and happy as any of the company present. In their nest are now five little children, too young and weak to fly, and there is no one to feed them or look after them."

"Oh, that is dreadful!" exclaimed Twinkle. "Can't Chubbins and I do something for the little goldfinches?"

"Why, that is why I was so anxious to find you," answered Policeman Bluejay. "You haven't laid any eggs yet, and have no one to depend upon you. So I hoped you would adopt the goldfinch babies."

"We will," said Chubbins, promptly. "We can feed them out of our basket."

"Oh, yes," chimed in the girl. "We couldn't catch grubs for them, you know."

"It won't be necessary," observed the policeman, with a sly wink at the eagle. "They're too young yet to know grubs from grub."

Chapter XI

The Orphans

The eagle now bade them good-bye and flew away in search of prey, while the bluejay and the child-larks directed their flight toward that part of the great forest where they lived.

"Are you sure the men have gone?" asked Chubbins.

"Yes," replied the policeman; "they left the forest as soon as they had shot Jolly Joe, for the brown bear was so heavy that they had to carry him on a pole resting across their shoulders. I hope they won't come again very soon."

"Did they take Mrs. Hootaway with them?" asked Twinkle.

"Yes; she will probably be stuffed, poor thing!"

Presently they passed near the rosy glow that lighted up the center of the forest with its soft radiance, and the girl said:

"That is the Paradise Land, where the Birds of Paradise live. The eagle has promised to ask one of those birds to let us visit their country."

"Oh, I can do better than that, if you wish to visit the Paradise," responded the bluejay; "for the Guardian of the Entrance is a special friend of mine, and will do whatever I ask him to."

"Will he, really?" asked the girl, in delight.

"To be sure. Some day I will take you over there, and then you will see what powerful friends Policeman Bluejay has."

"I'd like that," declared Twinkle.

Their swift flight enabled them to cover the remaining distance very rapidly, and soon they were at home again.

They first flew to the nest of the goldfinches, which was in a tree not far from the maple where the lark-children lived. There they found the tiny birds, who were yet so new that they were helpless indeed. Mrs. Redbreast was sitting by the nest when they arrived, and she said:

"The poor orphans are still hungry, although I have fed them all the insects I could find near. But I am glad that you have come, for it is time I was at home looking after my own little ones."

"Chubbins and I have 'dopted the goldfinches," said Twinkle, "so we will look after them now. But it was very nice of you, Mrs. Redbreast, to take care of them until we arrived."

"Well, I like to be neighborly," returned the pretty bird; "and as long as cruel men enter our forest no mother can tell how soon her own little ones will be orphaned and left helpless."

"That is true," said the policeman, nodding gravely.

So Mrs. Redbreast flew away and now Chubbins looked curiously into the nest, where several fluffy heads were eagerly lifted with their bills as wide open as they could possibly stretch.

"They must be just *awful* hungry, Twink," said the boy.

"Oh, they're always like that," observed Policeman Bluejay, calmly. "When anyone is around they open their mouths to be fed, whether they are hungry or not. It's the way with birdlets."

"What shall we feed them?" asked Twinkle.

"Oh, anything at all; they are not particular," said the bluejay, and then he flew away and left the child-larks to their new and interesting task.

"I'll be the father, and you be the mother," said Chubbins.

"All right," answered Twinkle.

"Peep! peep! peep!" said the tiny goldfinches.

"I wonder if the luncheon in our basket would agree with them," remarked the girl, looking at the open mouths reflectively as she perched her own brown body upon the edge of the deep nest.

"Might try it," suggested the boy. "The cop says they're not particular, and what's good enough for us ought to be good enough for them."

So they flew to where the basket hung among the thick leaves of the tree, which had served to prevent the men from discovering it, and crept underneath the cloth that covered it.

"Which do you think they'd like best," asked Chubbins, "the pickles or the cheese?"

"Neither one," Twinkle replied. "The sandwiches will be best for them. Wait; I'll pick out some of the meat that is between the slices of bread. They'll be sure to like that."

"Of course," agreed Chubbins, promptly. "They'll think it's bugs."

So each one dragged out a big piece of meat from a sandwich, and by holding it fast in one claw they managed to fly with the burden to the nest of the goldfinch babies.

"Don't give it to 'em all at once," cautioned the girl. "It would choke 'em."

"I know," said Chubbins.

He tore off a tiny bit of the meat and dropped it into one of the wide-open bills. Instantly it was gone and the mouth was open again for more. They tried to divide the dinner equally among them, but they all looked so alike and were so ravenous to eat everything that was dropped into their bills that it was hard work to keep track of which had been fed and which had not. But the child-larks were positive that each one had had enough to keep it from starving, because there was a big bunch in front of each little breast that was a certain proof of a full crop.

The next task of the guardians was to give the birdlets drink; so Twinkle and Chubbins flew to the brook and by hunting around a while they found an acorn-cup that had fallen from one of the oak trees. This they filled with water, and then Twinkle, who was a trifle larger than the boy-lark, clutched the cup firmly with her toes and flew back to the orphans without spilling more than a few drops. They managed to pour some of the water into each open mouth, and then Twinkle said:

"There! they won't die of either hunger or thirst in a hurry, Chub. So now we can feed ourselves."

"Their mouths are still open," returned the boy, doubtfully.

"It must be a habit they have," she answered. "Wouldn't you think they'd get tired stretching their bills that way?"

"Peep! peep! peep!" cried the baby goldfinches.

"You see," said the boy, with a wise look, "they don't know any better. I had a dog once that howled every time we shut him up. But if we let him alone he stopped howling. We'll go and get something to eat and let these beggars alone a while. Perhaps they'll shut their mouths by the time we get back again."

"Maybe," replied Twinkle.

They got their own luncheon from the basket, and afterward perched on the tree near the nest of the little goldfinches. They did not feel at all comfortable in their old nest in the maple, because they could not forget the tragic deaths of the inhabitants of the three hollows in the tree – the three "flats" as poor Wisk had merrily called them.

During the afternoon several of the birds came to call upon the orphans, and they all nodded approval when they found the child-larks watching over the little ones. Twinkle questioned some of the mothers anxiously about that trick the babies had of keeping their bills open and crying for food, but she was told to pay no attention to such actions.

Nevertheless, the pleadings of the orphans, who were really stuffed full of food, made the child-larks so nervous that they hailed with delight the arrival of

Policeman Bluejay in the early evening. The busy officer had brought with him Mrs. Chaffinch, a widow whose husband had been killed a few days before by a savage wildcat.

Mrs. Chaffinch declared she would be delighted to become a mother to the little goldfinches, and rear them properly. She had always had good success in bringing up her own children, she claimed, and the goldfinches were first cousins to the chaffinches, so she was sure to understand their ways perfectly.

Twinkle did not want to give up her charges at first, as she had become interested in them; but Chubbins heaved a sigh of relief and declared he was glad the "restless little beggars" had a mother that knew more about them than he did. The bluejay hinted that he considered the widow's experience would enable her to do more for the baby goldfinches than could a child-lark who had never yet laid an egg, and so Twinkle was forced to yield to his superior judgment.

Mrs. Chaffinch settled herself in a motherly manner upon the nest, and the two bird-children bade her good-night and returned to their own maple tree, where they had a rather wakeful night, because Chubbins thoughtlessly suggested that the place might be haunted by the ghosts of the grey owl, Wisk, and Mrs. 'Possum.

But either the poor things had no ghosts or they were too polite to bother the little child-larks.

Chapter XII

The Guardian

The next morning ushered in a glorious day, sunny and bright. The sky was a clear blue, and only a slight breeze ruffled the leaves of the trees. Even before Twinkle and Chubbins were awake the birds were calling merrily to one another throughout the forest, and the chipmunks chirped in their own brisk, businesslike way as they scuttled from tree to tree.

While the child-larks were finishing their breakfast Policeman Bluejay came to them, his feathers looking fresh and glossy and all his gorgeous colorings appearing especially beautiful in the sunshine.

"Today will be a rare day to visit the Paradise," he said; "so I have come to escort you to the Guardian of the Entrance, who I am sure will arrange for you to enter that wonderful country."

"It is very kind of you to remember our wish," said Twinkle. "We are all ready."

So they flew above the tree-tops and began their journey toward the center of the forest.

"Where's your p'liceman's hat and club?" Chubbins asked the bluejay.

"Why, I left them at home," was the reply. "I'm not on official duty today, you know, and the Guardian does not like to see anything that looks like a weapon. In his country there are no such things as quarrels or fighting, or naughtiness of any sort; for as they have everything they want there is nothing to quarrel over or fight for. The Birds of Paradise have laws, I understand; but they obey them because they are told to, and not because they are forced to. It would be a bad country for a policeman to live in."

"But a good place for everyone else," said Twinkle.

"Perhaps so," agreed the policeman, reluctantly. "But I sometimes think the goody-goody places would get awful tiresome to live in, after a time. Here in our part of the forest there is a little excitement, for the biggest birds only obey our laws through fear of punishment, and I understand it is just the same in the world of men. But in the Birds' Paradise there lives but one race, every member of which is quite particular not to annoy any of his fellows in any way. That is why they will admit no disturbing element into their country. If you are admitted, my dears, you must be very careful not to offend anyone that you meet."

"We'll try to be good," promised Chubbins.

"I would not dare to take any of my own people there," continued the bluejay, flying swiftly along as they talked together; "but you two are different, and more like the fairy Birds of Paradise themselves than like our forest birds. That is the reason I feel sure the Guardian will admit you."

"I'm naughty sometimes, and so is Chubbins," said Twinkle, honestly. "But we try not to be any naughtier than we can help."

"I am sure you will behave very nicely," replied the bluejay.

After a time the rosy glow appeared reflected in the blue sky, and as they flew toward it the soft and delightful radiance seemed to grow and deepen in intensity. It did not dazzle their eyes in the least, but as the light penetrated the forest and its furthest rays fell upon the group, they experienced a queer sense of elation and light-hearted joy.

But now the breeze freshened and grew more strong, pressing against their feathered breasts so gently yet powerfully that they soon discovered they were not advancing at all, but simply fluttering in the air.

"Drop down to the ground," whispered the bluejay; and they obeyed his injunction and found that close to the earth the wind was not so strong.

"That is a secret I learned some time ago," said their friend. "Most birds who seek to enter the Paradise try to beat against the wind, and are therefore always driven back; but there is just one way to approach the Guardian near enough to converse with him. After that it depends entirely upon his good-will whether you get any farther."

The wind still blew so strongly that it nearly took their breath away, but by creeping steadily over the ground they were able to proceed slowly, and after a time the pressure of the wind grew less and less, until it suddenly ceased altogether.

Then they stopped to rest and to catch their breaths, but before this happened Twinkle and Chubbins both uttered exclamations of amazement at the sight that met their eyes.

Before them was a grove composed of stately trees not made of wood, but having trunks of polished gold and silver and leaves of exquisite metallic colorings. Beneath the trees was a mass of brilliant flowers, exceedingly rare and curious in form, and as our little friends looked upon them these flowers suddenly began a chant of greeting and then sang a song so sweet and musical that the lark-children were entranced and listened in rapt delight.

When the song ended the flowers all nodded their heads in a pretty way, and Twinkle drew a long breath and murmured:

"Isn't it odd to hear flowers sing? I'm sure the birds themselves cannot beat that music."

"They won't try," replied the policeman, "for Birds of Paradise do not sing."

"How strange!" exclaimed the girl.

"The land they live in is so full of music that they do not need to," continued the bluejay. "But before us is the entrance, leading through the limbs of that great golden tree you see at the left. Fly swiftly with me, and perch upon the middle branch."

With these words he darted toward the tree, and Twinkle and Chubbins followed. In a few seconds they alighted upon the branch and found themselves face to face with the first Bird of Paradise they had yet seen.

He possessed a graceful carriage and a most attractive form, being in size about as large as a common pigeon. His eyes were shrewd but gentle in expression and his pose as he stood regarding the newcomers was dignified and impressive. But the children had little time to note these things because their wondering eyes were riveted upon the bird's magnificent plumage. The feathers lay so smoothly against his body that they seemed to present a solid surface, and in color they were a glistening emerald green upon the neck and wings, shading down on the breast to a softer green and then to a pure white. The main wing-feathers were white, tipped with vivid scarlet, and the white feathers of his crest were also tipped with specks of flame. But his tail feathers were the most beautiful of all his gay uniform. They spread out in the shape of a fan, and every other feather was brilliant green and its alternate feather snow white.

"How lovely!" cried Twinkle, and the bird bowed its head and with a merry glance from its eyes responded:

"Your admiration highly honors me, little stranger."

"This," said Policeman Bluejay, "is the important official called the Guardian of the Entrance of Paradise. Sir Guardian, permit me to introduce to you two children of men who have been magically transformed into skylarks against their will. They are not quite birds, because their heads retain the human shape; but whatever form they may bear, their natures are sweet and innocent and I deem them worthy to associate for a brief time with your splendid and regal race. Therefore I have brought them here to commend them to your hospitality and good-will, and I hope you will receive them as your guests."

"What are your names, little strangers?" asked the Guardian.

"Mama calls me Twinkle," said the girl.

"I'm Chubbins," said the boy.

The Guardian looked attentively at the bluejay.

"You know our regulations," said he; "no birds of the forest are admitted to our Paradise."

"I know," replied the policeman. "I will await my little friends here. It is pleasure enough for me to have just this glimpse of your beautiful fairyland."

The Guardian nodded his approval of this speech.

"Very well," he answered, "you shall remain and visit with me. If all forest birds were like you, my friend, there would be little danger in admitting them into our society. But they are not, and the laws must be regarded. As for the child-larks, I will send them first to the King, in charge of the Royal Messenger, whom I will now summon."

He tossed his head upward with an abrupt motion, and in the tree-top a chime of golden bells rang musically in the air. The flowers beneath them caught up the refrain, and sang it softly until another bird came darting through the air and alighted on the golden limb beside the Guardian.

The newcomer was differently garbed from the other. His plumage was orange and white, the crest and wing-feathers being tipped with bright blue. Nor was he so large as the Guardian, nor so dignified in demeanor. Indeed, his expression was rather merry and roguish, and as he saw the strangers he gave a short, sharp whistle of surprise.

"My dear Ephel," said the Guardian, "oblige me by escorting these child-larks to the presence of his Majesty the King."

"I am delighted to obey your request," answered Ephel the Messenger, brightly. Then, turning to Twinkle and Chubbins, he added: "I trust you will find my society agreeable during our flight to the royal monarch of Paradise."

Twinkle was too much embarrassed by this politeness to answer at once, but Chubbins said "Sure thing!" in a matter-of-fact voice, and the Messenger nodded gaily and continued:

"Then we will go, if it pleases you."

He spread his wings in a flash of color and sped away into the Paradise, and the children eagerly followed him.

Chapter XIII

The King Bird

More and more magnificence was unfolded as they advanced into this veritable fairyland of the birds. Vines of silver climbed up the golden trunks of trees and mingled their twining threads with the brilliant leaves. And now upon the trees appeared jeweled blossoms that sparkled most exquisitely in the rosy-hued radiance that, in this favored spot, had taken the place of sunshine. There were beds of plants with wide-spreading leaves that changed color constantly, one hue slowly melting into another and no two leaves on the same plant having the same color at the same time. Yet in spite of the vivid coloring that prevailed everywhere, each combination seemed in perfect harmony and served to delight the senses.

Bushes that emitted a grateful fragrance bore upon slender branches little bells that at times tinkled in the perfumed breeze and played sweet melodies, while here and there were clusters of fountain-lilies that shot sprays of crystal water high into the air. When the water fell back again and the drops struck against the broad leaves of the plants, they produced a melodious sound that was so delightful that Twinkle thought she could listen to it for hours.

Their guide flew silently on, and the two children were so much amazed by their surroundings that they had no words for questions or even remarks.

The scene was ever shifting and becoming more and more lovely and fascinating, and the paradise was more extensive than they had thought it.

By and bye Ephel the Messenger approached the central part, where was a great arbor thickly covered with masses of pure white flowers. Some of these were large, like chrysanthemums and mammoth white double roses, while among them were twined smaller and more delicate blossoms, like the bells of lilies-of-the-valley.

Ephel entered the arch of the arbor and flew on, for it was of great extent and continually enlarged from the point of entrance, so that at last the child-larks found themselves in a lofty circular chamber banked on sides and roof with solid masses of the snow-white flowers, which filled the air with a sweet and agreeable perfume. The floor was also a mass of white blossoms, so that the place resembled the inside of a huge cornucopia.

But the eyes of the little strangers were not directed so much to the arbor itself as to the group of splendid birds that occupied the flower-chamber and perched upon a wide-spreading bush of filigree gold that rose from the middle of the floor and spread its dainty branches in every direction.

On the lower branches sat many birds of marvelous colorings, some having blue the predominant tint in their feathers, and others green, or scarlet, or brilliant yellows. In strong contrast with these were a few modest-looking birds with soft brown feathers covering their graceful forms, that sat silently upon the lowest and most retired branch of the golden bush; but still greater was the contrast of all present with the magnificence of the one occupying the topmost branch.

This gorgeous creature, whose splendor dominated the white bower, at once won the children's attention, and they had no doubt they were gazing upon the King Bird of Paradise.

The feathers of his head and neck were so fine that they looked like a covering of velvet. These seemed to be, at first, of a delicate lavender color, but the children observed that they shone with a different tint at every movement the King made. The body feathers, also as glossy as velvet, were of a rich royal purple, shading to lavender and then to white upon his breast. His wing plumes were white, tipped with specks of lustrous gold.

But by far the most astonishing part of the King's plumage was that which consisted of the dainty, fern-like plumes that rose from his body and tail and spread in graceful and bewildering curves both right and left, until his form seemed to be standing in a feathery bower of resplendent beauty. All the colors of the rainbow were seen in these delicate feathers, and against the white background of the arch this monarch of the feathered world appeared more royally magnificent than any words can describe.

Both Twinkle and Chubbins gasped with amazement and delight as, at the command of Ephel, they alighted upon a lowly branch of the golden bush and bowed their heads before the ruler of the birds' fairyland.

"Ah, whom have we here?" asked the King, in a soft voice, as he strutted and proudly turned himself upon his perch.

"Strangers, your Majesty," answered the Messenger. "They are sent to you by the Guardian of the Entrance because they are gentle and innocent, and are neither birds nor mortals, but a part of both."

"They are certainly very curious," remarked the King, staring at the human heads upon the lark bodies. "May I ask you, little strangers, how you happen to exist in your present form?"

Twinkle, tossing her head to throw back a straggling lock of hair that had fallen across her eyes, began in her sweet voice to tell the story of their enchantment, and not only the King but all the Birds of Paradise present listened intently to her words.

When she had finished the King exclaimed:

"Indeed, my dear child-larks, you are worthy to be our guests in fairyland. So it will please me if you will be as happy and comfortable as possible, and enjoy your stay with us as much as you can. My people will delight to honor and amuse you, and Ephel shall continue to guide you wherever you go."

"Thank you," returned Twinkle, earnestly; and Chubbins added, in his blunt way: "Much obliged."

"But, before you go," continued his Majesty, "tell me what you think of my royal person. Am I not beautiful?"

"You are, indeed," replied Twinkle; "only –"

"Only what?" asked the King, as she hesitated.

"Only I'm sorry you are so vain, and strut around so, and want everyone to see how beautiful you are."

"Why should I not? Is not vanity one of the great virtues?" asked the King, in a surprised voice.

"My mama says people ought not to think themselves nice, or pretty," said the child. "With us, to be vain is a fault, and we are taught to be modest and unassuming."

"How remarkable!" exclaimed the King. "And how very thoughtless your mother must be. Here we think that if God creates us beautiful it is a sin not to glory in His work, and make everyone acknowledge the kindly skill of the Supreme Maker's hand. Should I try to make others think, or should I myself think, that I am not most gracefully formed and most gorgeously clothed, I would be guilty of the sin of not appreciating the favor of God, and deserve to be punished."

Twinkle was amazed, but could find no words to contradict this astonishing idea.

"I had not thought of it in that way," she answered. "Perhaps I am wrong, your Majesty; and certainly you are very beautiful."

"Think it over," said the King, graciously. "Learn to be grateful for every good thing that is yours, and proud that you have been selected by Nature for adornment. Only in this way may such rare favors be deserved. And now the royal Messenger will show you the sights of our Paradise, and try to entertain you pleasantly while you are our guests."

He turned aside, with these words, and fluttered his waving feathers so that their changing tints might dazzle the eyes of all observers. But immediately afterward he paused and cried out:

"Dear me! One of my wing plumes is disarranged. Help me, you ladies!"

At once the small brown birds on the lower branches, who had been modestly quiet because they had no gay plumage, flew up to the King and with their bills skillfully dressed his feathers, putting the wing plume into its place again and arranging it properly, while the other birds looked on with evident interest.

As the lark-children turned away to follow the Messenger Chubbins remarked:

"I'm glad *I* haven't got all those giddy feathers."

"Why?" asked Twinkle, who had been rather awed by the King's splendor.

"Because it would take all my time to keep 'em smooth," answered the boy. "The poor King can't do much more than admire himself, so he don't get time to have fun."

Chapter XIV

A Real Fairyland

As they left the royal arbor of white flowers the Messenger turned to the left and guided his guests through several bright and charming avenues to a grove of trees that had bright blue bark and yellow leaves. Scattered about among the branches were blossoms of a delicate pink color, shaped like a cup and resembling somewhat the flower of the morning-glory.

"Are you hungry?" asked Ephel.

"Oh, I could eat something, I guess," said Chubbins.

The Messenger flew to one of the trees and alighted upon a branch where three of the pink, cup-shaped flowers grew in a row. The children followed him, and sitting one before each blossom they looked within the cups and found them filled with an unknown substance that both looked and smelled delicious and appetizing.

"It is royal amal," said their guide, busily pecking at his cup with his bill. "Help yourselves, little ones. You will find it very nice indeed."

"Well," said Twinkle, "I'd be glad to eat it if I could. But it wouldn't do Chubbins and me a bit of good to stick our noses into these cups."

Ephel turned to look at them.

"True," he remarked; "it was very careless of me to forget that you have no bills. How are you accustomed to eat?"

"Why, with spoons, and knives and forks," said the girl.

"You have but to ask for what you need," declared the royal Messenger.

Twinkle hesitated, scarcely knowing what to say. At last she spoke boldly: "I wish Chub and I had spoons."

Hardly had the words left her lips when two tiny golden spoons appeared in the flower-cups. Twinkle seized the spoon before her in one claw and dipped up a portion of the strange food, which resembled charlotte russe in appearance. When she tasted it she found it delicious; so she eagerly ate all that the blossom contained.

When she looked around for Chubbins she found he was gone. He had emptied his cup and carried the golden spoon to another blossom on a higher limb, where the girl discovered him eating as fast as he could dip up the food.

"Let us go to another tree," said Ephel. "There are many excellent things to eat, and a variety of food is much more agreeable than feasting upon one kind."

"All right," called Chubbins, who had succeeded in emptying the second cup.

As they flew on Twinkle said to the guide:

"I should think the blossoms would all be emptied in a little while."

"Oh, they fill up again in a few moments," replied Ephel. "Should we go back even now, I think we would find them all ready to eat again. But here are the conona bushes. Let us taste these favorite morsels."

The bushes on which they now rested had willow-green branches with silver balls growing thickly upon them. Ephel tapped lightly upon one of the balls with his bill and at once it opened by means of a hinge in the center, the two halves of the ball lying flat, like plates. On one side Twinkle found tiny round pellets of cake, each one just big enough to make a mouthful for a bird. On the other side was a thick substance that looked like jelly.

"The proper thing to do," said their guide, "is to roll one of the pellets in the jelly, and then eat it."

He showed Twinkle how to do this, and as she had brought her golden spoon with her it was easy enough. Ephel opened a ball for Chubbins and then one for himself, and the children thought this food even nicer than the first they had eaten.

"Now we will have some fruit," declared the Messenger. He escorted his charges to an orchard where grew many strange and beautiful trees hanging full of fruits that were all unknown to the lark-children. They were of many odd shapes and all superbly colored, some gleaming like silver and gold and others being cherry-red or vivid blue or royal purple in shade. A few resembled grapes and peaches and cherries; but they had flavors not only varied and delicious but altogether different from the fruits that grow outside of the Birds' Paradise.

Another queer thing was, that as fast as the children ate one fruit, another appeared in its place, and they hopped from branch to branch and tree to tree, trying this one and that, until Chubbins exclaimed:

"Really, Twink, I can't eat another mouthful."

"I'm afraid we've both been stuffing ourselves, Chub," the girl replied. "But these things taste so good it is hard to stop at the right time."

"Would you like to drink?" asked Ephel.

"If you please," Twinkle answered.

"Then follow me," said the guide.

He led them through lovely vistas of wonderful trees, down beautiful winding avenues that excited their admiration, and past clusters of flowering plants with leaves as big as umbrellas and as bright as a painter's palette. The Paradise seemed to have been laid out according to one exquisite, symmetrical plan, and although the avenues or paths between the trees and plants led in every direction, the ground beneath them was everywhere thickly covered with a carpet of magnificent flowers or richly tinted ferns and grasses. This was because the birds never walked upon the ground, but always flew through the air.

Often, as they passed by, the flowers would greet them with sweet songs or choruses and the plants would play delightful music by rubbing or striking their leaves against one another, so that the children's ears were constantly filled with harmony, while their eyes were feasted on the bewildering masses of rich color, and each breath they drew was fragrant with the delicious odors of the blossoms that abounded on every side.

"Of all the fairylands I've ever heard of or read about," said Twinkle, "this certainly is the best."

"It's just a peach of a fairyland," commented Chubbins, approvingly.

"Here is the nectar tree," presently remarked the royal Messenger, and he paused to allow them to observe it.

The tree was all of silver – silver trunk and branches and leaves – and from the end of each leaf or branch dripped sparkling drops of a pink-tinted liquid. These glistened brightly as they fell through the air and lost themselves in a bed of silver moss that covered all the ground beneath the tree.

Ephel flew to a branch and held his mouth open so that a drop from above fell into it. Twinkle and Chubbins followed his example, and found the pink liquid very delightful to drink. It seemed to quench their thirst and refresh them at the same time, and when they flew from the queer dripping tree they were as light-hearted and gay as any two children so highly favored could possibly have felt.

"Haven't you any water in your paradise?" asked the little girl-lark.

"Yes, of course," Ephel answered. "The fountain-lilies supply what water we wish to drink, and the Lustrous Lake is large enough for us all to bathe in. Besides these, we have also the Lake of Dry Water, for you must know that the Lustrous Lake is composed of wet water."

"I thought all water was wet," said Chubbins.

"It may be so in your country," replied the Royal Messenger, "but in our Paradise we have both dry and wet water. Would you like to visit these lakes?"

"If you please," said Twinkle.

Chapter XV

The Lake of Dry Water

They flew through the jeweled gardens for quite a way, emerging at last from among the trees to find before them a pretty sheet of water of a greenish hue. Upon the shore were rushes that when swayed by the breeze sang soft strains of music.

"This," announced their guide, "is the Lake of Dry Water."

"It *looks* wet, all right," said Chubbins, in a tone of doubt.

"But it isn't," declared Ephel. "Watch me, if you please."

He hovered over the lake a moment and then dove downward and disappeared beneath the surface. When he came up again he shook the drops of water from his plumage and then flew back to rejoin his guests.

"Look at me," he said. "My feathers are not even damp." They looked, and saw that he spoke truly. Then Chubbins decided to try a bath in the dry water, and also plunged into the lake. When he came to the surface he floated there for a time, and ducked his head again and again; but when he came back to the others not a hair of his head nor a feather of his little brown body was in the least moist.

"That's fine water," said the boy-lark. "I suppose you Birds of Paradise bathe here all the time."

"No," answered Ephel; "for only wet water is cleansing and refreshing. We always take our daily baths in the Lustrous Lake. But here we usually sail and disport ourselves, for it is a comfort not to get wet when you want to play in the water."

"How do you sail?" asked Twinkle, with interest.

"I will show you," replied their guide.

He flew to a tall tree near, that had broad, curling leaves, and plucked a leaf with his bill. The breeze caught it at once and wafted it to the lake, so that it fell gently upon the water.

"Get aboard, please," called Ephel, and alighted upon the broad surface of the floating leaf. Twinkle and Chubbins followed, one sitting in front of their guide and one behind him. Then Ephel spread out his wings of white and orange, and the breeze pushed gently against them and sent the queer boat gliding over the surface of the dry water.

"Sometimes, when the wind is strong," said the Royal Messenger, "these frail craft upset, and then we are dumped into the water. But we never mind that, because the water is dry and we are not obliged to dress our feathers again."

"It is very convenient," observed Twinkle, who was enjoying the sail. "Could one be drowned in this lake?"

"I suppose an animal, like man, could, for it is as impossible to breathe beneath dry water as it is beneath wet. But only birds live here, and they cannot drown, because as soon as they come to the surface they fly into the air."

"I see," said Twinkle, musingly.

They sailed way across the lake, and because the wind was gentle they did not upset once. On reaching the farther shore they abandoned the leaf-boat and again took wing and resumed their flight through the avenues.

There was a great variety of scenery in the Paradise, and wherever they went something new and different was sure to meet their view.

At one place the avenue was carpeted with big pansies of every color one could imagine, some of them, indeed, having several colors blended together upon their petals. As they passed over the pansies Twinkle heard a chorus of joyous laughter, and looking downward, she perceived that the pansies all had faces, and the faces resembled those of happy children.

"Wait a minute," she cried to Chubbins and the guide, and then she flew downward until she could see the faces more plainly. They smiled and nodded to the girl-lark, and laughed their merry laughter; but when she spoke to them Twinkle found they were unable to answer a single word.

Many of the faces were exceedingly beautiful; but others were bold and saucy, and a few looked at her with eyes twinkling with mischief. They seemed very gay and contented in their paradise, so Twinkle merely kissed one lovely face that smiled upon her and then flew away to rejoin her companions.

Chapter XVI

The Beauty Dance

Before long they came to another and larger sheet of water, and this Twinkle decided was the most beautiful lake she had ever seen. Its waters were mostly deep blue in color, although they had a changeable effect and constantly shifted from one hue to another. Little waves rippled all over its surface, and the edges of the waves were glistening jewels which, as they scattered in spray and fell into the bosom of the lake, glinted and sparkled with a thousand flashing lights. Here were no rushes upon the shore, but instead of them banks of gorgeous flowers grew far down to the water's edge, so that the last ones dipped their petals into the lake itself.

Nestling upon this bank of flowers the Royal Messenger turned to his companions and said:

"Here let us rest for a time, while I call the friendly fishes to entertain you."

He ended his speech with a peculiar warble, and at its sound a score of fishes thrust their heads above the surface of the water. Some of them were gold-fish and some silver-fish, but others had opal tints that were very pretty. Their faces were jolly in expression and their eyes, Chubbins thought, must be diamonds, because they sparkled so brightly.

Swimming softly here and there in the lovely waters of the Lustrous Lake, the fishes sang this song:

"We are the fishes of the lake;
Our lives are very deep;
We're always active when awake
And quiet when asleep.

"We get our fins from Finland,
From books we get out tales;
Our eyes they come from Eyerland
And weighty are our scales.

"We love to flop and twist and turn
Whenever 'tis our whim.
Yet social etiquette we learn
Because we're in the swim.

"Our beds, though damp, are always made;
We need no fires to warm us;
When we swim out we're not afraid,
For autos cannot harm us.

"We're independent little fish
And never use umbrellas.
We do exactly as we wish
And live like jolly fellows."

As the fishes concluded their song they leaped high into the air and then plunged under the water and disappeared, and it was hard to tell which sparkled most brilliantly, their gold and silver bodies or the spray of jewels they scattered about them as they leaped.

"If you should dive into this lake," said Ephel the Messenger, "your feathers would be dripping wet when you came out again. It is here we Birds of Paradise bathe each morning, after which we visit the Gleaming Glade to perform our Beauty Dance."

"I should like to see that glade," said Twinkle, who was determined to let nothing escape her that she could possibly see.

"You shall," answered Ephel, promptly. "We will fly there at once."

So he led the way and presently they entered a thicker grove of trees than any they had before noticed. The trunks were so close together that the birds could only pass between then in single file, but as they proceeded in this fashion it was not long before they came to a circular space which the child-lark knew at once must be the Gleaming Glade.

The floor was of polished gold, and so bright that as they stood upon it they saw their forms reflected as in a mirror. The trees surrounding them were also of gold, being beautifully engraved with many attractive designs and set with rows of brilliant diamonds. The leaves of the trees, however, were of burnished silver, and bore so high a gloss that each one served as a looking-glass, reproducing the images of those standing in the glade thousands of times, whichever way they chanced to turn.

The gleam of these mirrorlike leaves was exceedingly brilliant, but Ephel said this radiance was much stronger in the morning, when the rosy glow of the atmosphere was not so powerful.

"Then," said he, "the King Bird and all the Nobility of Paradise, who rejoice in the most brilliant plumage, come here from their bath and dance upon the golden floor the Beauty Dance, which keeps their blood warm until the feathers have all dried. While they dance they can admire their reflections in the mirrors, which adds greatly to their pleasure."

"Don't they have music to dance by?" asked Chubbins.

"Of course," the Messenger replied. "There is a regular orchestra that plays exquisite music for the dance; but the musicians are the female Birds of Paradise, who, because their plumage is a modest brown, are not allowed to take part in the Beauty Dance."

"I think the brown birds with the soft grey breasts are just as pretty as the gaily clothed ones," said Twinkle. "The male birds are too bright, and tire my eyes."

Ephel did not like this speech, for he was very proud of his own gorgeous coloring; but he was too polite to argue with his guest, so he let the remark pass.

"You have now witnessed the most attractive scenes in our favored land," he said; "but there are some curious sights in the suburbs that might serve to interest you."

"Oh! have you suburbs, too?" she asked.

"Yes, indeed. We do not like to come into too close contact with the coarse, outer world, so we have placed the flying things that are not birds midway between our Paradise and the great forest. They serve us when we need them, and are under our laws and regulations; but they are so highly favored by being permitted to occupy the outer edge of our glorious Paradise that they willingly obey their masters. After all, they live happy lives, and their habits, as I have said, may amuse you.

"Who are they?" enquired Chubbins.

"Come with me, and you shall see for yourselves."

They flew away from the grove of the Gleaming Glade and Ephel led them by pleasant routes into a large garden with many pretty flowers in it. Mostly it was filled with hollyhocks – yellow, white, scarlet and purple.

Chapter XVII

The Queen Bee

As they approached they heard a low, humming sound, which grew louder as they advanced and aroused their curiosity.

"What is it?" asked Twinkle, at last.

Ephel answered: "It is the suburb devoted to the bees."

"But bees are not birds!" exclaimed Twinkle.

"No; as I have told you, the suburbs contain flying things that cannot be called birds, and so are unable to live in our part of the Paradise. But because they have wings, and love all the flowers and fruits as we do ourselves, we have taken them under our protection."

Ephel perched upon a low bush, and when the child-larks had settled beside him he uttered a peculiar, shrill whistle. The humming sound grew louder, then, and presently hundreds of great bees rose above the flower tops and hovered in the air. But none of them approached the bush except one monstrous bumblebee that had a body striped with black and gold, and this one sailed slowly toward the visitors and alighted gracefully upon a branch in front of them.

The bee was all bristling with fine hairs and was nearly half as big as Twinkle herself; so the girl shrank back in alarm, and cried:

"Oh-h-h! I'm afraid it will sting me!"

"How ridiculous!" answered the bee, laughing in a small but merry voice. "Our stings are only for our enemies, and we have no enemies in this Paradise; so we do not use our stingers at all. In fact, I'd almost forgotten I had one, until you spoke."

The words were a little mumbled, as if the insect had something in its mouth, but otherwise they were quite easy to understand.

"Permit me to introduce her Majesty the Queen Bee," said their guide. "These, your highness, are some little child-larks who are guests of our King. I have brought them to visit you."

"They are very welcome," returned the Queen Bee. "Are you fond of honey?" she asked, turning to the children.

"Sometimes," replied Chubbins; "but we've just eaten, and we're chock full now."

"You see," the Queen remarked, "my people are all as busy as bees gathering the honey from every flower."

"What do you do with it?" asked Twinkle.

"Oh, we eat part of it, and store up the rest for a rainy day."

"Does it ever rain here?" enquired Chubbins.

"Sometimes, at night, when we are all asleep, so as to refresh and moisten the flowers, and help them to grow."

"But if it rains at night, there can't be any rainy days," remarked Twinkle; "so I can't see the use of saving your honey."

"Nor can I," responded the Queen, laughing again in her pleasant way. "Out in the world people usually rob us of our stores, and so keep us busy getting more. But here there are not even robbers, so that the honey has been accumulating until we hardly know what to do with it. We have built a village of honeycombs, and I have just had my people make me a splendid palace of honey. But it is our way to gather the sweet stuff, whether we need it or not, so we have to act according to our natures. I think of building a mountain of honey next."

"I'd like to see that honey palace," said Twinkle.

"Then come with me," answered the Queen Bee, "for it will give me pleasure to show it to you."

"Shall we go?" asked the girl-lark, turning to Ephel.

"Of course," he returned. "It is quite a wonderful sight, and may interest you."

So they all flew away, the Queen Bee taking the lead, and passed directly over the bed of flowers with its swarm of buzzing, busy bees.

"They remind me of a verse from 'Father Goose,'" said Twinkle, looking curiously but half fearfully at the hundreds of big insects.

"What is the verse?" asked the Queen.

"Why, it goes this way," answered the girl:

"'A bumble-bee was buzzing on a yellow hollyhock
When came along a turtle, who at the bee did
mock,
Saying "Prithee, Mr. Bumble, why make that
horrid noise?
It's really distracting, and everyone annoys."

""""I'm sorry," said, quite humble, the busy droning
bee,
"The noise is just my bumble, and natural, you see.
And if I didn't buzz so I'm sure that you'll agree
I'd only be a big fly, and not a bumble-bee.""""

"That is quite true," said the bee, "and describes our case exactly. But you should know that we are not named 'bumblebees' by rights, but 'Humble Bees.' The latter is our proper name."

"But why 'humble?'" asked Twinkle.

"Because we are common, work-a-day people, I suppose, and not very aristocratic," was the reply. "I've never heard why they changed our name to 'bumble,' but since you recited that verse I imagine it is on account of the noise our wings make."

They had now passed over the flower beds and approached a remarkable village, where the houses were all formed of golden-yellow honey-combs. There were many pretty shapes among these houses, and some were large and many stories in height while others were small and had but one story. Some had spires and minarets reaching up into the air, and all were laid out into streets just like a real village.

But in the center stood a great honey-comb building with so many gables and roofs and peaks and towers that it was easy to guess it was the Queen Bee's palace, of which she had spoken.

They flew in at a second-story window and found themselves in a big room with a floor as smooth as glass. Yet it was composed of man six-sided cells filled with honey, which could be seen through the transparent covering. The walls and roof were of the same material, and at the end of the room was a throne shaped likewise of the honey cells, like everything else. On a bench along the wall sat several fat and sleepy-looking bumble-bees, who scarcely woke up when their queen entered.

"Those are the drones," she said to her visitors. "It is useless to chide them for their laziness, because they are too stupid to pay attention to even a good scolding. Don't mind them in any way."

After examining the beautiful throne-room, they visited the sleeping chambers, of which there were many, and afterward the parlors and dining room and the work-rooms.

In these last were many bees building the six-sided pockets or cells for storing the honey in, or piling them up in readiness for the return of those who were gathering honey from the flowers.

"We are not really honey-bees," remarked the Queen; "but gathering honey is our chief business, after all, and we manage to find a lot of it."

"Won't your houses melt when it rains?" asked Twinkle.

"No, for the comb of the honey is pure wax," the Queen Bee replied. "Water does not melt it at all."

"Where do you get all the wax?" Chubbins enquired.

"From the flowers, of course. It grows on the stamens, and is a fine dust called pollen, until we manufacture it into wax. Each of my bees carries two sacks, one in front of him, to put the honey in, and one behind to put the wax in."

"That's funny," said the boy-lark.

"I suppose it may be, to you," answered the Queen, "but to us it is a very natural thing."

Chapter XVIII

Good News

Ephel and the children now bade the good-natured Queen Bee good-bye, and thanked her for her kindness. The Messenger led them far away to another place that he called a "suburb," and as they emerged from a thick cluster of trees into a second flower garden they found the air filled with a great assemblage of butterflies, they being both large and small in size and colored in almost every conceivable manner.

Twinkle and Chubbins had seen many beautiful butterflies, but never such magnificent ones as these, nor so many together at one time. Some of them had wings fully as large as those of the Royal Messenger himself, even when he spread them to their limit, and the markings of these big butterfly wings were more exquisite than those found upon the tail-feathers of the proudest peacocks.

The butterflies paid no attention to their visitors, but continued to flutter aimlessly from flower to flower. Chubbins asked one of them a question, but got no reply.

"Can't they talk?" he enquired of Ephel.

"Yes," said the Messenger, "they all know how to talk, but when they speak they say nothing that is important. They are brainless, silly creatures, for the most part, and are only interesting because they are beautiful to look at. The King likes to watch the flashes of color as they fly about, and so he permits them to live in this place. They are very happy here, in their way, for there is no one to chase them or to stick pins through them when they are caught."

Just then a chime of bells tinkled far away in the distance, and the Royal Messenger listened intently and then said:

"It is my summons to his Majesty the King. We must return at once to the palace."

So they flew into the air again and proceeded to cross the lovely gardens and pass through the avenues of jeweled trees and the fragrant orchards and groves until they came at last to the royal bower of white flowers.

The child-larks entered with their guide and found the gorgeous King Bird of Paradise still strutting on his perch on the golden bush and enjoying the admiring glances of his courtiers and the ladies of his family. He turned as the children entered and addressed his Messenger, saying:

"Well, my dear Ephel, have you shown the strangers all the sights of our lovely land?"

"Most of them, your Majesty," replied Ephel.

"What do you think of us now?" asked the King, turning his eyes upon the lark-children.

"It must be the prettiest place in all the world!" cried Twinkle, with real enthusiasm.

His Majesty seemed much pleased. "I am very sorry you cannot live here always," he said.

"I'm not," declared Chubbins. "It's too pretty. I'd get tired of it soon."

"He means," said Twinkle, hastily, for she feared the blunt remark would displease the kindly King, "that he isn't really a bird, but a boy who has been forced to wear a bird's body. And your Majesty is wise enough to understand that the sort of life you lead in your fairy paradise would be very different from the life that boys generally lead."

"Of course," replied the King. "A boy's life must be a dreadful one."

"It suits me, all right," said Chubbins.

The King looked at him attentively.

"Would you really prefer to resume your old shape, and cease to be a bird?" he asked.

"Yes, if I could," Chubbins replied.

"Then I will tell you how to do it," said the King. "Since you told me your strange story I have talked with my Royal Necromancer, who knows a good deal about magic, and especially about that same tuxix who wickedly transformed you in the forest. And the Royal Necromancer tells me that if you can find a tingle-berry, and eat it, you will resume your natural form again. For it is the one antidote in all the world for the charm the tuxix worked upon you."

"What *is* a tingle-berry?" asked Twinkle, anxiously, for this information interested her as much as it did Chubbins.

"I do not know," said the King, "for it is a common forest berry, and never grows in our paradise. But doubtless you will have little trouble in finding the bush of the tingle-berry when you return to the outside world."

The children were both eager to go at once and seek the tingle-berry; but they could not be so impolite as to run away just then, for the King announced that he had prepared an entertainment in their honor.

So they sat on a branch of the golden bush beside their friend Ephel, while at a nod from the King a flock of the beautiful Birds of Paradise flew into the bower and proceeded to execute a most delightful and bewildering set of aërial evolutions. They flew swiftly in circles, spirals, triangles, and solid squares, and all the time that they performed sweet music was played by some unseen band. It almost dazzled the eyes of the child-larks to watch this brilliant flashing of the colored wings of the birds, but the evolutions only lasted for a few minutes, and then the birds flew out again in regular ranks.

Then the little brown lady-birds danced gracefully upon the carpet, their dainty feet merely touching the tips of the lovely flowers. Afterward the flowers themselves took part, and sang a delightful chorus, and when this was finished the King said they would now indulge in some refreshment.

Instantly a row of bell-shaped blossoms appeared upon the golden bush, one for each bird present, and all were filled with a delicious ice that was as cold and refreshing as if it had just been taken from a freezer. Twinkle and Chubbins asked for spoons, and received them quickly; but the others all ate the ices with their bills.

The King seemed to enjoy his as much as anyone, and Twinkle noticed that as fast as a blossom was emptied of its contents it disappeared from the branch.

The child-larks now thanked the beautiful but vain King very earnestly for all his kindness to them, and especially for telling them about the tingle-berries; and when all the good-byes had been exchanged Ephel flew with them back to the tree where they had left the Guardian of the Entrance and their faithful comrade, Policeman Bluejay.

Chapter XIX

The Rebels

They were warmly greeted by the bluejay, who asked: "Did you enjoy the wonderful Paradise?"

"Very much, indeed," cried Twinkle. "But we were sorry you could not be with us."

"Never mind that," returned the policeman, cheerfully. "I have feasted my eyes upon all the beauties visible from this tree, and my good friend the Guardian has talked to me and given me much good advice that will surely be useful to me in the future. So I have been quite contented while you were gone."

The children now gave their thanks to Ephel for his care of them and polite attention, and the Royal Messenger said he was pleased that the King had permitted him to serve them. They also thanked the green-robed Guardian of the Entrance, and then, accompanied by Policeman Bluejay, they quitted the golden tree and began their journey back to the forest.

It was no trouble at all to return. The wind caught their wings and blew against them strongly, so that they had but to sail before the breeze and speed along until they were deep in the forest again. Then the wind moderated, and presently died away altogether, so that they were forced to begin flying in order to continue their journey home.

It was now the middle of the afternoon, and the policeman said:

"I hope all has been quiet and orderly during my absence. There are so many disturbing elements among the forest birds that I always worry when they are left alone for many hours at a time."

"I'm sure they have behaved themselves," returned Twinkle. "They fear your power so much that the evil-minded birds do not dare to offend you by being naughty."

"That is true," said the policeman. "They know very well that I will not stand any nonsense, and will always insist that the laws be obeyed."

They were now approaching that part of the forest where they lived, and as the policeman concluded his speech they were surprised to hear a great flutter of wings among the trees, and presently a flock of big black rooks flew toward them.

At the head of the band was a saucy-looking fellow who wore upon his head a policeman's helmet, and carried under his wing a club.

Policeman Bluejay gave a cry of anger as he saw this, and dashed forward to meet the rooks.

"What does this mean, you rascal?" he demanded, in a fierce voice.

"Easy there, my fine dandy," replied the rook, with a hoarse laugh. "Don't get saucy, or I'll give you a rap on the head!"

The rooks behind him shrieked with delight at this impudent speech, and that made the mock policeman strut more absurdly than ever.

The bluejay was not only astonished at this rebellion but he was terribly angry as well.

"That is my policeman's helmet and club," he said sternly. "Where did you get them?"

"At your nest, of course," retorted the other. "We made up our minds that we have had a miserable bluejay for a policeman long enough; so the rooks elected me in your place, and I'm going to make you birds stand around and obey orders, I can tell you! If you do as I command, you'll get along all right; if you don't, I'll pound you with your own club until you obey."

Again the rooks screamed in an admiring chorus of delight, and when the bluejay observed their great numbers, and that they were all as large as he was, and some even larger and stronger, he decided not to risk an open fight with them just then, but to take time to think over what had best be done.

"I will call the other birds to a meeting," he said to the rook, "and let them decide between us."

"That won't do any good," was the reply. "We rooks have decided the matter already. We mean to rule the forest, after this, and if any one, or all of the birds, dare to oppose us, we'll fight until we force them to serve us. Now, then, what do you intend to do about it?"

"I'll think it over," said Policeman Bluejay.

"Oho! oho! He's afraid! He's a coward!" yelled the rooks; and one of them added:

"Stand up and fight, if you dare!"

"I'll fight your false policeman, or any one of you at a time," replied the bluejay.

"No, you won't; you'll fight us all together, or not at all," they answered.

The bluejay knew it would be foolish to do that, so he turned away and whispered to the lark-children:

"Follow me, and fly as swiftly as you can."

Like a flash he darted high into the air, with Twinkle and Chubbins right behind him, and before the rooks could recover from their surprise the three were far away.

Then the big black birds gave chase, uttering screams of rage; but they could not fly so swiftly as the bluejay and the larks, and were soon obliged to abandon the pursuit.

When at last he knew that they had escaped the rooks, Policeman Bluejay entered the forest again and went among the birds to call them all to a meeting. They obeyed the summons without delay, and were very indignant when they heard of the rebellion of the rooks and the insults that had been heaped upon their regularly elected officer. Judge Bullfinch arrived with his head bandaged with soft feathers, for he had met the rook policeman and, when he remonstrated, had been severely pounded by the wicked bird's club.

"But what can we do?" he asked. "The rooks are a very powerful tribe, and the magpies and cuckoos and blackbirds are liable to side with them, if they seem to be stronger than we are."

"We might get all our people together and fall upon them in a great army, and so defeat them," suggested an oriole.

"The trouble with that plan," decided the judge, "is that we can only depend upon the smaller birds. The big birds might desert us, and in that case we would be badly beaten."

"Perhaps it will be better to submit to the rooks," said a little chickadee, anxiously. "We are neither warriors nor prizefighters, and if we obey our new rulers they may leave us in peace."

"No, indeed!" cried a linnet. "If we submit to them they will think we are afraid, and will treat us cruelly. I know the nature of these rooks, and believe they can only be kept from wickedness by a power stronger than their own."

"Hear me, good friends," said the bluejay, who had been silent because he was seriously thinking; "I have a plan for subduing these rebels, and it is one that I am sure will succeed. But I must make a long journey to accomplish my purpose. Go now quietly to your nests; but meet me at the Judgment Tree at daybreak tomorrow morning. Also be sure to ask every friendly bird of the forest to be present, for we must insist upon preserving our liberty, or else be forever slaves to these rooks."

With these words he rose into the air and sped swiftly upon his errand.

The other birds looked after him earnestly.

"I think it will be well for us to follow his advice," said Judge Bullfinch, after a pause. "The bluejay is an able bird, and has had much experience. Besides, we have ever found him just and honorable since the time we made him our policeman, so I feel that we may depend upon him in this emergency."

"Why, it is all we can do," replied a robin; and this remark was so true that the birds quietly dispersed and returned to their nests to await the important meeting the next morning.

Chapter XX

The Battle

Twinkle and Chubbins flew slowly home to their nests in the maple tree, pausing to ask every bird they met where tingle-berries grew. But none of them could tell.

"I'm sorry we did not ask Policeman Bluejay," said Chubbins.

"I intended to ask him, but we hadn't time," replied Twinkle. "But he will be back tomorrow morning."

"I wonder what he's going to do," remarked the boy.

"Don't know, Chub; but it'll be the right thing, whatever it is. You may be sure of that."

They visited the nest of the baby goldfinches, and found the Widow Chaffinch still caring for the orphans in her motherly way. The little ones seemed to be as hungry as ever, but the widow assured the lark-children that all five had just been fed.

"Did you ever hear of a tingle-berry?" asked Twinkle.

"Yes; it seems to me I have heard of that berry," was the reply. "If I remember rightly my grandmother once told me of the tingle-berries, and warned me never to eat one. But I am quite certain the things do not grow in our forest, for I have never seen one that I can recollect."

"Where do they grow, then?" enquired Chubbins.

"I can't say exactly where; but if they are not in the forest, they must grow in the open country."

The child-larks now returned to their own nest, and sat snuggled up in it during the evening, talking over the day's experiences and the wonderful things they had seen in the fairylike Paradise of the Birds. So much sight-seeing had made them tired, so when it grew dark they fell fast asleep, and did not waken until the sun was peeping over the edge of the trees.

"Good gracious!" exclaimed the girl, "we shall be late at the meeting at the Judgment Tree. Let's hurry, Chub."

They ate a hasty breakfast from the contents of their basket, and after flying to the brook for a drink and a dip in the cool water they hurried toward the Judgment Tree.

There they found a vast assemblage of birds. They were so numerous, indeed, that Twinkle was surprised to find that so many of them inhabited the forest.

But a still greater surprise was in store for her, for immediately she discovered sitting upon the biggest branch of the tree twenty-two bluejays, all in a row. They were large, splendidly plumaged birds, with keen eyes and sharp bills, and at their head was the children's old friend, the policeman.

"These are my cousins," he said to the child-larks, proudly, "and I have brought them from another forest, where they live, to assist me. I am not afraid of the foolish rooks now, and in a moment we shall fly away to give them battle."

The forest birds were all in a flutter of delight at the prompt arrival of the powerful bluejays, and when the word of command was given they all left the tree and flew swiftly to meet the rooks.

First came the ranks of the twenty-two bluejays, with the policeman at their head. Then followed many magpies and cuckoos, who were too clever to side with the naughty rooks when they saw the powerful birds the bluejay had summoned to his assistance. After these flew the smaller birds, of all descriptions, and they were so many and at the same time so angry that they were likely to prove stubborn foes in a fight.

This vast army came upon the rooks in an open space in the forest. Without waiting for any words or explanations from the rebels, the soldierly bluejays fell upon their enemies instantly, fighting fiercely with bill and claw, while the other birds fluttered in the rear, awaiting their time to join in the affray.

Policeman Bluejay singled out the rook which had stolen his helmet and club, and dashed upon him so furiously that the black rebel was amazed, and proved an easy victim to the other's superior powers. He threw down the club and helmet at once; but the bluejay was not satisfied with that, and attacked the thief again and again, until the air was full of black feathers torn from the rook's body.

After all, the battle did not last long; for the rooks soon screamed for mercy, and found themselves badly plucked and torn by the time their assailants finally decided they had been punished enough.

Like all blustering, evil-disposed people, when they found themselves conquered they whined and humbled themselves before the victors and declared they would never again rebel against Policeman Bluejay, the regularly appointed guardian of the Law of the Forest. And I am told that after this day the rooks, who are not rightly forest birds, betook themselves to the nearest villages and farm houses, and contented themselves with plaguing mankind, who could not revenge themselves as easily as the birds did.

After the fight Policeman Bluejay thanked his cousins and sent them home again, and then the birds all surrounded the policeman and cheered him gratefully for his cleverness and bravery, so that he was the hero of the hour.

Judge Bullfinch tried to make a fine speech, but the birds were too excited to listen to his words, and he soon found himself without an audience.

Of course, Twinkle and Chubbins took no part in the fight, but they had hovered in the background to watch it, and were therefore as proud of their friend as any of the forest birds could be.

Chapter XXI

The Tingle-Berries

When the excitement of the morning had subsided and the forest was quiet again, Policeman Bluejay came to the nest of the child-larks, wearing his official helmet and club. You may be sure that one of the first things Twinkle asked him was if he knew where tingle-berries grew.

"Of course," he replied, promptly. "They grow over at the north edge of the forest, in the open country. But you must never eat them, my dear friend, because they are very bad for birds."

"But the Royal Necromancer of the King Bird of Paradise says the tingle-berries will restore us to our proper forms," explained the girl.

"Oh; did he say that? Then he probably knows," said the bluejay, "and I will help you to find the berries. We birds always avoid them, for they give us severe pains in our stomachs."

"That's bad," observed Chubbins, uneasily.

"Well," said Twinkle, "I'd be willing to have a pain or two, just to be myself again."

"So would I, if it comes to that," agreed the boy. "But I'd rather have found a way to be myself without getting the pain."

"There is usually but one thing that will overcome an enchantment," remarked the bluejay, seriously; "and if it is a tingle-berry that will destroy the charm which the old tuxix put upon you, then nothing else will answer the same purpose. The Royal Necromancer is very wise, and you may depend upon what he says. But it is late, at this season, for tingle-berries. They do not grow at all times of the year, and we may not be able to find any upon the bushes."

"Cannot we go at once and find out?" asked Twinkle, anxiously.

"To be sure. It will grieve me to lose you, my little friends, but I want to do what will give you the most happiness. Come with me, please."

They flew away through the forest, and by and by came upon the open country to the north, leaving all the trees behind them.

"Why, this is the place we entered the forest, that day we got 'chanted!" cried Twinkle.

"So it is," said Chubbins. "I believe we could find our way home from here, Twink."

"But we can't go home like we are," replied the girl-lark. "What would our folks say, to find us with birds' bodies?"

"They'd yell and run," declared the boy.

"Then," said she, "we must find the tingle-berries."

The bluejay flew with them to some bushes which he said were the kind the tingle-berries grew upon, but they were all bare and not a single berry could be found.

"There must be more not far away," said the policeman, encouragingly. "Let us look about us."

They found several clumps of the bushes, to be sure; but unfortunately no berries were now growing upon them, and at each failure the children grew more and more sad and despondent.

"If we have to wait until the bushes bear again," Twinkle remarked, "it will be nearly a year, and I'm sure we can't live in the forest all winter."

"Why not?" asked the policeman.

"The food in our basket would all be gone, and then we would starve to death," was the reply. "We can't eat bugs and worms, you know."

"I'd rather die!" declared Chubbins, mournfully.

The bluejay became very thoughtful.

"If we could find some of the tingle bushes growing near the shade of the forest," he said at last, "there might still be some berries remaining on them. Out here in the bright sunshine the berries soon wither and drop off and disappear."

"Then let us look near the trees," suggested Twinkle.

They searched for a long time unsuccessfully. It was growing late, and they were almost in despair, when a sharp cry from Policeman Bluejay drew the child-larks to his side.

"What is it?" enquired the girl, trembling with nervous excitement.

"Why," said the policeman, "here is a bush at last, and on it are exactly two ripe tingle-berries!"

Chapter XXII

The Transformation

They looked earnestly at the bush, and saw that their friend spoke truly. Upon a high limb was one plump, red berry, looking much like a cranberry, while lower down grew another but smaller berry, which appeared to be partially withered.

"Good!" the lark-children cried, joyfully; and the next moment Chubbins added: "You eat the big berry, Twink."

"Why?" she asked, hesitating.

"It looks as if it had more stomach-ache in it," he replied.

"I'm not afraid of that," said she. "But do you suppose the little berry will be enough for you? One side of it is withered, you see."

"That won't matter," returned the boy-lark. "The Royal Necromancer said to eat one berry. He didn't say a little or a big one, you know, or whether it should be plump or withered."

"That is true," said the girl-lark. "Shall I eat mine now?"

"The sooner the better," Chubbins replied.

"Don't forget me, little friend, when you are a human again," said Policeman Bluejay, sadly.

"I shall never forget you," Twinkle answered, "nor any part of all your kindness to us. We shall be friends forever."

That seemed to please the handsome blue bird, and Twinkle was so eager that she could not wait to say more. She plucked the big, plump berry, put it in her mouth with her little claw, and ate it as soon as possible.

In a moment she said: "Ouch! Oo-oo-oo!" But it did not hurt so badly, after all. Her form quickly changed and grew larger; and while Chubbins and Policeman Bluejay watched her anxiously she became a girl again, and the bird's body with its soft grey feathers completely disappeared.

As she felt herself changing she called: "Good-bye!" to the bluejay; but even then he could hardly understand her words.

"Good-bye!" he answered, and to Twinkle's ears it sounded like "Chir-r-rip-chee-wee!"

"How did it feel?" asked Chubbins; but she looked at him queerly, as if his language was strange to her, and seemed to be half frightened.

"Guess I'll have to eat my berry," he said, with a laugh, and proceeded to pluck and eat it, as Twinkle had done. He yelled once or twice at the cramp the fruit gave him, but as soon as the pain ceased he began to grow and change in the same way his little comrade had.

But not entirely. For although he got his human body and legs back again, all in their natural size, his wings remained as they were, and it startled him to find that the magic power had passed and he was still partly a bird.

"What's the matter?" asked Twinkle.

"Is anything wrong?" enquired the bluejay.

The boy understood them both, although they could not now understand each other. He said to Twinkle:

"I guess the berry wasn't quite big enough." Then he repeated the same thing in the bird language to Policeman Bluejay, and it sounded to Twinkle like:

"Pir-r-r-r – eep – cheep – tweet!"

"What in the world can you do?" asked the girl, quite distressed. "It will be just dreadful if you have to stay like that."

The tears came to Chubbins' eyes. He tried to restrain them, but could not. He flapped his little wings dolefully and said:

"I wish I was either one thing or the other! I'd rather be a child-lark again, and nest in a tree, than to go home to the folks in this way."

Policeman Bluejay had seen his dilemma at the first, and his sharp eyes had been roving over all the bushes that were within the range of his vision. Suddenly he uttered a chirp of delight and dashed away, speedily returning with another tingle-berry in his bill.

"It's the very last one there is!" said he to Chubbins.

"But it is all that I want," cried the boy, brightening at once; and then, regardless of any pain, he ate the berry as greedily as if he was fond of a stomach-ache.

The second berry had a good effect in one way, for Chubbins' wings quickly became arms, and he was now as perfectly formed as he had been before he met with the cruel tuxix. But he gave a groan, every once in a while, and Twinkle suspected that two berries were twice as powerful as one, and made a pain that lasted twice as long.

As the boy and girl looked around they were astonished to find their basket standing on the ground beside them. On a limb of the first tree of the forest sat silently regarding them a big blue bird that they knew must be Policeman Bluejay, although somehow or other he had lost his glossy black helmet and the club he had carried underneath his wing.

"It's almost dark," said Twinkle, yawning. "Let's go home, Chub."

"All right."

He picked up the basket, and for a few minutes they walked along in silence.

Then the boy asked:

"Don't your legs feel heavy, Twink?"

"Yes," said she; "do yours?"

"Awful," said he.

www.ingramcontent.com/pod-product-compliance
Lightning Source LLC
Chambersburg PA
CBHW030414310726
48979CB00002B/413

* 9 7 8 1 4 6 3 8 9 6 0 6 5 *